THE RIBBON KEY

BY

JULIE ANN JAMES

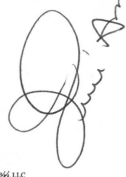

the PeppertreePress, LLC
Sarasota, Florida

For information regarding permission,
call 941-922-2662 or contact us at our website:
www.peppertreepublishing.com or write to:
the Peppertree Press, LLC.
Attention: Publisher
1269 First Street, Suite 7
Sarasota, Florida 34236

ISBN: 978-1-61493-700-5

Library of Congress Number: 2020901009

Printed September 2020

To my cousin Joe – Just Be-"Cuz"

Great mystery....Kept me turning pages.

I have not had a lot of opportunity to sit and read a book in a long time. I ordered this book and LOVED it. So now I'm going to see what other titles she has available.

—Wendi L.

Enjoyed this mystery from start to finish.

Easy reading and keeps you intrigued until the very end! I highly recommend this book!

—Shelley B.

Best thriller in awhile!

This book is very well written. That kept me reading it straight through! I really hope this becomes a series due the nature of the characters and the plot. Loved all the twists! So good!! Fun thriller to read on a rainy day.

—Dennis O.

// Peter woke up at sunrise still with the tainted letter in his grasp, his fingers holding on so tight, they were beginning to turn a not so healthy shade of blue. It was the black and white of the words that spoke the truth."

Peter Foster

// She never realized how much inner strength she had as she kicked, screamed, and tried to scratch any part of the crazed psychopath's body she could reach. She missed all but once, the feeling satisfying as her finger-nails came in contact with this faceless maniac's skin, digging in deep and gliding down hard as if she was moving in slow motion across a chalk board."

Kerry Ann Hoffman

CHAPTER ONE

The salty breeze swept across the wraparound porch of the cottage house on Briggs Way where Peter Foster sat alone on the Adirondack swing for the first time since his wife went missing and now presumed dead. It has been several days now and still no sign of finding his beloved Kate.

He rocked mindlessly back and forth all while staring out onto the Atlantic Ocean, his sad brown eyes mesmerized by the hypnotic movement and sound of the waves crashing onto the shoreline.

A constant flow of tears rolled down his face involuntarily, giving him pause on occasion to wipe them off and make some sort of effort to stop them from pouring out. Realizing he had no control of his emotions at this time—who would in such a situation as this—this nightmare of his wife's disappearance was something that happened to the other guy, not to him and his immediate family. This was something you read about in the newspaper or see on the six o'clock news. Of course, you are touched by this sad and tragic news and perhaps make an empathic comment for that person and family and then move on with the thoughts of what's for dinner or on television later that night. But when the news is about your family and the reality sets in and the pain is literally in your face every long grueling twenty-four-hour day that it painstakingly fills you up from the air inside your lungs, to the thoughts in your mind down to the deepest emotions of your soul.

For now, he had no choice but to force his body to go through the motions of this day-to-day, moment-to-moment he was living in, even though his mind was numb as to what he was doing from each passing moment to the next. He had to snap himself out of it and talk to himself out loud in some instances, just to put one foot in front of the other.

His sister Mary was kind enough to come to Chatham and be by his side for the past few weeks. However, he convinced her that he would be fine and so she packed her suitcase and drove her Ford Focus back to Rhode Island. He assured her that he would keep her informed of any news from the authorities the moment he heard a word.

His sister was eight years younger and still had two teenage kids at home who needed their mom. He loved his sister, but it was time for her to leave, as there was nothing she could do for him.

"I am capable of opening a can of soup with no problem, Sis," he would say to her in jest to lighten the mood and to make her feel less guilty.

He could see it in her eyes that she was ready to go home, even though she pleaded with him to stay for a few more days. The eyes are always a dead giveaway, regardless of how hard you try to be sincere. In his experience of sixty plus years, with most people—it is just something that they say to make themselves feel better. Make the offer, however, in secret hope the person lets you off the hook. He did just that and now she is almost home and happy about it. He appreciated her help and support, however, now he had to reflect on his tragic loss and try to recover and help the police and detectives catch this son-of-a-bitch that abducted his wife.

He must have been sitting on the swing for hours as he took notice that the sun had set quite some time ago and now the stars were making an appearance and lighting up the clear night sky.

He was still hopeful that Bentley, their beloved golden retriever would somehow find his way back home. He had to be a witness to Kate's abduction as he never left her side in his three years on this earth. She would sometimes trip over him by accident, because he was always under foot. She didn't seem to mind and would just keep on doing what she was doing regardless of the big hairy red head at her feet. He was positive that Bentley was with her that dreadful day. They were running partners, the dynamic duo some of the neighbors would call them. Kate had trained him since he was a puppy to run beside her, and for him as long as he was with her that was all that mattered. They would get up at 6:30 a.m. and together head out the front door feet and paws to the pavement, and run the streets of this quiet quaint little town of Chatham.

It wasn't until just a few weeks ago Kate had met a new friend on her running path. Kerry Ann Hoffman was in her early fifties, newly single and looking for Mr. Right and so far only to find a few Mr. Wrongs. She and Kate had a common thread of running and became fast friends. He recalled Kate mentioning the night before that Kerry Ann wasn't able to run that morning as she had an appointment and would meet up with her and Bentley the next day. He couldn't help but wonder if she had been questioned by the police or if they even knew about her. He found it odd that she hadn't called the house asking about Kate's whereabouts. He had met her briefly at the beach and then a casual wave between them when he would see the trio running along the side of the road. Maybe she wasn't comfortable with him and under the circumstances decided to keep her distance. For the time being, he was willing to give her the benefit of the doubt, however, making certain to bring up her name to the detectives the next time they came nosing around the house.

He pushed himself up from the swing and steadied himself before turning around to step inside the house as he was feeling weak and undernourished, as food was not a priority.

He held himself up by leaning in on the doorframe between the porch and the living room or what she described as the fireplace room and then crossed his arms over his blue-and-white checked shirt, now untucked and hanging out of his khaki shorts.

Most of the furniture was still covered with crisp white cotton sheets. She insisted repeatedly that it kept the dust from forming on the fabric. It was one of her many pet peeves before closing up their vacation home for the winter months. Everything had to be neat as a pin. He couldn't help but to think if they had left one day earlier, Kate would still be here with him where she belonged. He was certain of that. God only knows where she is and if she is still alive.

No matter how hard he tried to divert his eyes, they would automatically shoot over in that horrific direction.

The blood stain on the carpet in front of the fireplace had been cleaned and scrubbed what seemed like hundreds of times. However, no matter how many times he looked over at where the stain used to be, he could still see it in his mind. He recalled his personal endeavor, being down on all fours scrubbing the light-color carpeting, his hands in a fist and his skin raw from rug burn from the constant friction. He couldn't help but think about Kate and how much she would hate— no, despise—that there was such a horrendous spot on what she referred to as her "good carpet." She would call out to him no matter where she was in the house the moment he stepped one foot into the room and yelled out, "Keep your muddy shoes off my *good carpet.*"

Without fail she would insist on wiping off Bentley's paws, even if he was just on the porch for a few minutes. He didn't seem to mind and would give her kisses while she worked diligently on each dirty paw and then after a quick inspection, give him a pat on the head and tell him to step lightly.

He envisioned the blood from her wounds had seeped down into the fibers of the carpet and onto the padding and as far down as the concrete slab. He couldn't bear the thought of how terrified his wife of thirty years must have been if the intruder maybe now has killed her for whatever reason he still could not figure out. Somehow she found the strength to try and get away, bleeding and running for her life. He was still trying to figure out how this person got inside the house. He must have followed her or perhaps she knew him, as there was no sign of forced entry and there wasn't anything missing. And where was Bentley at that time? Why didn't he protect her and where are they now? Maybe he killed his dog, too—maybe they are both dead.

CHAPTER TWO

He was relieved to see that the newspaper journalists and television crews had packed up their gear and moved to, rumor had it, Pleasant Bay Beach—now the prime location to report any and all leads that happened to wash up on shore. To Peter, Pleasant Beach was not so pleasant in his mind.

Although the detectives had vacated the scene at his house, he knew they were close by, hovering over him like that annoying hum of a mosquito in the room that you wanted to swat but couldn't see. He knew he was on a short leash and not considered a suspect. However, it wouldn't take long for them to come knocking, because no matter where the evidence lead them, the spouse was at all times considered to be the number one suspect. In his mind she was missing but in their minds, they had her dead and buried.

He stepped out on the side porch to drink his morning coffee—something he and Kate did together many mornings. No matter where they sat at this house the views were beautiful.

The population of Chatham was small and for the most part everyone was friendly. He did feel some uneasy stares to the back of his head on one or two occasions in the past couple of days, however, nobody was pointing fingers—not yet anyway.

He and Kate loved this town and talked about moving here permanently. However, they were still teetering with the idea and would push the thought to the side and make a comment like, "maybe next year" or "let's talk about it after the holidays."

Since they were never able to have children, nothing was stopping them from making the move other than themselves. Both retired educators, so they were set with a nest egg they would have been able to live on for the rest of their lives.

There were steps as wide as the porch that spilled out onto the lush backyard and a small deck large enough to fit a barn table and benches, fire pit, and a grill. Sheltering it was a cedar pergola Peter made with his own hands for a special birthday surprise for his lovely bride. He would never forget the expression on her face as her eyes filled with happy tears followed by a warm embrace for her handy man for giving her such an amazing gift. He would do anything for his Kate, anything to bring that smile he loved so much to her face. The pergola was indeed the perfect venue for entertaining, as they would have his sister and her family up quite often. His stomach turned the more he thought about it. What would be the point of having it now if his wife was dead? It would be all for nothing and there would be no more celebrations.

He sat down on the first step, took his glasses off, and then buried his face in his hands rubbing his eyes as they burned from the pollen in the air—maybe it was just the tiredness. He then placed the earpiece of his glasses in the corner of his mouth and chewed on the end—a nervous habit he was certain he would never kick.

He scanned the yard taking note of how beautiful it looked and all of Kate's and his efforts had paid off, from the fertilizer to the constant watering. It was worth spending the extra cash on the water bill so he could see Kate's face light up as he bragged about her talented green thumb to complete strangers or anyone that happened to pass by their house. With anything and everything she touched, it would bloom and turned into something spectacular.

The trees in the yard were stately and had to be at least a hundred years old, give or take a few years. There was an old beat-up tire swing tied to the lowest branch that Mary's boys loved to horse around on. Bentley would bark at them and try to bite their shoes as they swayed back and forth, teasing him and laughing at the game they created. The boys sure got a kick out of that, but it was mostly Bentley's joy. He could swear that Bentley was smiling the entire time. This was a memory he knew he would hold onto forever.

He took another sip of his coffee, sat it down on the step, and looked back out at the swing. He noticed that there was something sitting in the grass a couple of feet beyond the tire swing. Maybe it was a bag of mulch or soil that Kate had left there and forgotten about. He squinted for a bit, cleaned off his smudged lenses with the corner of his shirt, and placed them on his face to take a closer look.

He stood up and then with caution in his movements walked down the steps and into the yard. He squatted down in the grass and then whistled twice, followed by, "Come here, boy."

CHAPTER THREE

He laid him down on the kitchen floor his eighty-pound body was limp, which made him feel that much heavier.

In a hurried panic, Peter yanked open almost every drawer in the kitchen, his mind clouded of which one had the hand towels. He turned on the faucet and soaked one of the towels and squatted down next to his weak exhausted dog and squeezed the water out of the towel and into his mouth. He then used it to wipe off his face and then his eyes, which were swollen and red. He watched Bentley swallow the water which was a good sign he was going to be okay.

He ran his hands over his body, legs, and paws to see if he felt any broken bones or any open wounds. Bentley looked up at his owner with such love and admiration and sense of relief that he found his way home.

"Where is Kate, boy? Where is your mama? You need to take me to her, boy." Knowing that was a futile question, he then buried his head into Bentley's matted fur and sobbed. They comforted each other for a little while. Peter was feeling hopeless and helpless—his heart aching with a pain he had never felt before.

Bentley didn't move at all, as he seemed to enjoy the attention Peter was giving him. He gently pulled off what seemed like hundreds of burrs that were matted in Bentley's fur. He then removed his collar and laid it down on the floor next to him. He recalled how proud Kate was of that collar as she ordered it from one of those specialty magazines for runners and had it inscribed with the words, "Running is for dogs 2" and, of course, she had his name engraved on the bone-shaped dog tag. Kate was crazy about Bentley—they were crazy about each other.

Bentley popped his head up and issued a low growl. His attention was now directed toward the front door, however, Peter heard nothing.

"Well, you must be feeling better—that's great to see. Next on the docket for you, a bath."

It was a matter of a few seconds later and the doorbell rang. Peter pushed himself up from the hard surface, his knees hurting a bit from being on them for so long. He scooped up Bentley's collar and for the first time noticed there was something tied to it. He shoved it into his pocket, deciding to take a closer look later.

He opened the door, expecting the unexpected. Standing on the porch was a man in his mid-forties, buzz cut, and trim in stature. His badge on his belt loop was a dead giveaway to who he was, however, he introduced himself anyway.

He removed his Aviators and extended his hand. "Detective Ben Murphy," he said.

Peter took one look at this detective and could see it in his eyes even before he said another word.

"I need to talk with you, Mr. Foster."

He shook his hand and invited him inside. He then turned around to take a look at Bentley. He was up on all fours on the ready.

"Detective Murphy, is it? I don't recognize you as one of the detectives on this case. And from the reaction and behavior I am getting from my dog, he doesn't seem to like you much."

He was still standing in the doorway, as he was not feeling welcome from the dog and hadn't received an invitation to pass through the threshold. He shifted his weight nervously from side to side searching for the words to appease the man.

"I never did like dogs much, so your dog probably senses that—dogs are smart. I suppose we should give them more credit."

"You mean *you* should give them credit. Isn't that right, detective?"

The man looked down at his shoes and then Peter motioned for him to step inside.

"You have ten minutes to say what you need to say. No disrespect, but I have to tend to my dog, as he has been under a lot of stress."

"Mr. Foster, you are correct, I am not from around here. My jurisdiction is north of Chatham, close to Pleasant Bay. I have some unfortunate news to give you today. Is there someone here with you or perhaps someone I can call for you?"

Peter sat on the arm of the sofa and took in a deep breath preparing to hear what he had been dreading to hear all these weeks. Why from this guy? He didn't understand, as he had never met him before and didn't trust him.

"No, I am by myself, and I am a little taken back with you coming to my house without an escort from the local police department. Nonetheless, just give it to me straight, detective."

"Your wife was found on the beach yesterday afternoon. She is dead, Mr. Foster. We have just identified her as the missing woman from Chatham."

"Do you know who found her? Do you know who found my wife, Kate?" He stammered his words a bit, however managed to put his question out there as the color drained from his face.

"For the most part, the waters are shallow at the Pleasant Bay beach and always loaded with kayakers. They frequently stop by this beach to picnic and stretch their legs. It didn't take long for someone to spot her lying there face down in the sand. I am sorry, but I don't know their names, just that they were kayaking and stopped at the beach."

"Okay, enough, I am not ready to hear anymore just yet." Peter stood up from the arm of the sofa and put both hands on top of his head and then paced the floor.

"I know this is difficult, Mr. Foster, however, there is something else I wanted to share with you."

"What is it, detective?"

"There were two more women missing."

"You just said *were*?"

"Yes, that's what I meant to say. Their bodies were found this morning on the same beach."

CHAPTER FOUR

It was another sleepless night for Kerry Ann as every noise that resonated within the walls of her one-bedroom apartment sent her two feet off the floor. Hell, even her own shadow made her heart race.

She finally turned off the television as she was more than sick and tired of hearing the sad news about her friend Kate's abduction and now her murder. She wondered if the guilt that she was feeling would or could eventually kill her. Was it possible to die from guilt? She knew how ridiculous that sounded in her head and wished in more ways than one that she would have been with Kate on that fateful day she went missing. Maybe together they could have stopped this lunatic.

Kerry Ann intended to go straight to the police right after she found out that Kate was missing, and more so after she heard the tragic news that she was dead. She didn't have anything to share with the authorities, seeing that she didn't know Kate Foster that well, other than she was an avid runner and was married for many years to the same man and vacationed in Chatham for the summer months. Their discussions went as deep and far as health and fitness and Kate's personal priority of finding a guy for her to date. There weren't any red flags that alerted her that Kate had some deep-seated secrets she was holding onto. Nonetheless, most average people, male or female, are holding onto some secrets within their own minds taking them all the way to the grave, six feet under.

In the past few days she had been having nightmares and feeling as though she was being watched through the window of her apartment and to and from her office. One night she could swear someone was standing over her bed as she woke up in a cold sweat. She did her best to push the paranoia out of her head and blamed it on the news media. And why not? They ate this sort of stuff for breakfast and literally milked this type of news 24/7. She knew anyone could be next.

Kerry Ann made herself an English muffin, brushed her teeth, and then headed out the front door. Her office was close by, however, not quite walking distance.

She was the owner of a small, but lucrative marketing company and her expertise in the field helped her clients' businesses grow at a fast pace beyond where they would be in a five-year plan. Her clients were loyal, which was a win-win.

She pulled into the alley behind the stand-alone building and parked her sedan in one of the three available parking spots. She then keyed the lock to the small hole-in-the-wall office space, flipped on the light, and then plopped down in her desk chair.

It was a one-woman show and she preferred it that way. She managed the day-to-day, called the shots for herself, and offered the personal touch to her clients. And it worked.

She listened to her messages and then answered a few

emails. Then again, the longer she worked, the more she could feel the anxiety rising. At this point, it was time to make the call—to call Peter Foster and give him her condolences, if nothing else.

She didn't know Peter at all personally, other than what she heard second-hand from Kate. Kate would share a few antecdotes about their vacations over the pond and what they were having for dinner. On the other hand, she kept things about her husband private.

Kerry was more than dreading this call and now after all this time had passed by, she felt maybe it was too late and he wouldn't give her the time of day. What kind of friend does this? He had to think she was a terrible person. What if he thinks the worst—that she had something to do with her death? Regardless, she had to get it over with.

She found the number in her cell phone under Kate's home and hit **SEND**. She closed her eyes in anticipation, and on the second ring an unfamiliar voice answered by giving his name.

"Hello, this is Peter Foster."

"Peter, hello. This is Kerry Ann Hoffman—Kate's friend. I wanted to start off this conversation by letting you know how deeply sorry I am for your loss. I can't even imagine what you are going through."

"I know who you are. It's a little late for condolences, don't you think, Ms. Hoffman?"

She could feel her body start to overheat from the inside out and leaned her body on the corner of her desk.

"Peter, I realize I have not been considerate and should have called a long time ago. Is it possible that we meet for coffee today, if you have some time?"

"Why—do you have information about my wife's murder?"

"No, actually I don't. I just thought we could talk about what happened and maybe it would help somehow heal the wounds of missing her so much. Could you meet in say thirty minutes at the Chatham Perk—you know the place?"

Peter checked his watch and gave a quick answer.

"Yes, I can meet you ... see you there."

Kerry Ann ended the call, her hands trembling. She wasted no time at all and locked the front door before one of her clients bombarded her time. She didn't want to be late for this meeting. She grabbed her purse, throwing it over her shoulder, and tucked her cell phone into her back pocket. Car keys in hand, she was ready to go.

She started her sedan, adjusted the rearview mirror, and took in a deep breath, feeling a bit relieved, but at the same time nervous to meet Peter. Suddenly, she felt a hand cover her mouth and heard a man's voice as he pulled in close to her ear. Her eyes widened as she listened to his strident demands.

"You didn't lock your car—how could you be so irresponsible? Haven't you been watching the news? I have one word for you—drive!"

CHAPTER FIVE

Peter chose a booth for two in the far corner of the café, where he would be able to hear over the annoying reverberation of the latte machines and coffee grinders. It was bad enough he had to listen to the staff behind the counter attempt to enunciate the customers' names to the point of ridiculousness. He used to be able to tune things out like this, however, since the love of his life had been ripped from this earth, his attitude had shifted drastically.

He drummed his fingers on the high-gloss tabletop, all while keeping a watchful eye on the front door for a tall blonde to enter. Although a stranger to him, nonetheless, she had been a friend to his late wife, and for that, he would give her a few minutes to say whatever it is she felt the need to say.

To pass the time, he took inventory of the specialty coffees, teas, and novelty items for sale on the shelf and noticed a sign above that read, "Come on in out of the Grind." All of this was mindless nonsense and wasn't enough to divert his attention from thinking about his beautiful Kate. Today his heart was heavy and thoughts of the horrific and tragic way she died was beyond excruciating.

He checked his wrist for the time and then the clock on the wall behind the coffee counter—both were in agreement that Ms. Hoffman was running fifteen minutes late. Maybe this was the norm for her as he didn't know her traits. She could be one of those people that would always arrive late, apologize for being late, only to repeat her bad habit the next meeting. Regardless, it didn't matter much as he had nothing better to do, other than to wait out the investigation and plan his wife's memorial service.

He shifted his body as the seat wasn't exactly comfortable. As he reached into his jacket pocket and pulled out his cell phone, spilling onto the floor was Bentley's leather collar. He had completely forgotten about it being in his pocket until now and that there was something tied to it. When it landed on the hard surface, it made a sound as if a coin had dropped.

He picked it up to take a closer look and discovered it was a key attached to a ribbon. He had never given it much thought until now, as he remembered Kate standing in the kitchen late one night, threading this ribbon through the tiny holes of the house key. He could assume she conjured up this idea in the middle of the night, so she wouldn't have to drag along the bulky set. He could envision her beautiful face light up with excitement as she tossed the key over her head and tucked it safely inside her shirt before her early morning run. She took one look at him and said, "Ta Da," and flashed that warm smile in his direction—that smile that made him melt and fall in love with her all over again. This was a heartwarming memory he would always cherish.

His thoughts came rushing in as to how in the hell did this

ribbon that was around his wife's neck end up all twisted up in Bentley's collar. It made no sense to him.

He began the monotonous task of untangling it when his chore was interrupted by the deep voice of a stranger, but not whom he was anticipating.

"Mind if I sit here?" the stranger asked politely.

Peter glanced up at the gentleman staring down at him and then went back to the task at hand, while stating an assumption. "You have that look about you, if you don't mind me saying. You look similar to the man that stopped by my house first thing this morning—not in stature, but in demeanor. If I would take a stab in the dark, I would guess you are a detective with a notebook full of questions looking for answers."

"Interesting choice of words, Mr. Foster, and well done I might add. Your stab in the dark was accurate indeed."

"I have a sixth sense when it comes to people—it's a gift really. And since you know who I am, perhaps you could enlighten me with your name?"

The detective motioned to the seat and then squeezed himself into the small quarters, while tossing his business card on the table.

"It's Jake, Jake Elliot. I am a homicide detective with the Chatham Police Department. Most folks around here call me 'Big Jake' for obvious reasons."

"Did you find my wife's killer, Big Jake?"

"First and foremost, I am very sorry for your loss, Mr. Foster. And to answer your difficult question, I wish it was that simple as that would certainly make our job a hell of a lot easier. Cut and dried—but that's not the case. I did speak with the coroner's office and sadly your wife was strangled, just like the other two victims. I am deeply sorry to have to share this with you as it must come as a blow.

Peter sank deeper into the leather seat and turned his head away, wiping the tears from his cheeks and doing his best to process the detective's unfortunate blunt delivery.

"You know as I mentioned a detective stopped by my house this morning. Like you he flashed his credentials and wanted to tell me about the two other victims. I have to say, I didn't like this guy very much and neither did my dog. There was something about him that rubbed me the wrong way."

"What's his name, Mr. Foster?"

"He said his name was Ben Murphy and he worked for the Pleasant Bay Police Department. He knew the person that found my wife on the beach."

The detective sat back in the seat and folded his hands behind his head. Suddenly he sat up straight again ready to deliver his answer, which by his facial expression didn't appear to be good news.

"Mr. Foster, I have been a detective in Chatham for over thirty years and nothing slips by me. I know everyone that works at the police department from the basement to the top floor. I cannot tell you who showed up at your doorstep this morning, but I can guarantee that there is not a detective or even a mail clerk by the name of Ben Murphy who works in that office!"

CHAPTER SIX

Peter had been waiting for over an hour for Kerry Ann to show up at the coffeehouse and after two phone calls and several text messages with no response, he decided that he had enough and he had more important things to do.

He tossed a few bucks on the table for his coffee and then followed the detective out the door and onto the street where they both said their goodbyes and then headed in opposite directions. Peter barely made it to the corner when the detective stopped him with one more question.

"Mr. Foster, just one more thing, if you don't mind."

Peter turned around and waited for that one more thing.

"I would appreciate you coming down to the station later today and give my partner a description of this Ben Murphy character that paid you a visit at your residence. Would that be possible?"

The detective could see from Mr. Foster's expression that he had no reason to not be cooperative and do as he asked.

"Yes, of course, detective. I will be there around 3:00, if that works for your schedule?"

"Good. Thank you. I will let my partner know that you are coming and I will be there as well to introduce you. With your description, she will do a composite sketch in fine detail from the obvious scars down to the smallest freckle. I have to say I am looking forward to getting a visual of this guy. He is most likely telling the truth of who he is, however, one can never be too cautious."

Peter arrived home in less than twenty minutes, where he was greeted by a happy and well-rested Bentley. He set his keys down on the entryway table, as well as Bentley's collar, still a work in progress. Now he was ready to give an excited Bentley a proper hello.

"Hey, Buddy, you are looking bright-eyed," he said, patting him on the head.

"Come on, bud, let's go outside."

Together they walked to the back porch, Bentley moving his paws double-time, excited for Peter to open the screen door so he could chase whatever was scurrying around in the yard. Peter made sure the screen door was left propped open, so Bentley could come and go as he pleased. Once Bentley chased the pests out of the yard, he loved sitting out in the grass enjoying the sunlight and sniffing the air. He could take one look at Bentley's eyes and knew he *so* wanted to tell him what happened down to the finest of details. He had to have known, he had to have been there with Kate when it happened.

He let Bentley stay outside and enjoy the fresh air and stepped back inside the house, as his mind was on other things. He turned on both his computer and the television hitting the remote until it landed on the local station. In his mind, it was time to stop waiting for answers and start searching for himself. He didn't trust anyone at this point who could give him the answers that he wanted to know about his wife's murder, down to the last unbelievable detail. And who was this Ben Murphy character—why would he be nosing around his house and why did he have to deliver the unfortunate news without anyone else present to back him up? Maybe "Big Jake" was mistaken—or are we both wrong and this Murphy detective is legit … definitely time to do some digging.

Peter typed his name into the browser and waited it out. The internet connection wasn't exactly high-speed, so while his computer spun out of control he turned to watch the news.

The spunky news anchor he had grown accustomed to seeing on a daily basis popped up on the screen. Her warm smile, whether it was genuine or not, just made him feel better for some odd reason.

Behind her on the green screen was what he considered a low-budget graphic of a crime scene tape and silhouette of a body lying on the ground. It was done in poor taste, but recognizable of the topic she was about to broadcast. She had his full attention at this point, so he turned up the volume.

He listened intently to every word she said, processing the ridiculous title he was assuming the news media had conjured up to label the murderer of his beloved wife and the other two victims who have yet to be identified. They were making it sound like this predator had earned a lead role in a play at the local community theater. He could only hope that the psychopathic killer wasn't watching and relishing in his attention that he so did not deserve.

A few seconds later a photo of a young woman appeared on the screen with a phone number to call if anyone who was watching had any information as to her whereabouts. It seems the authorities found the missing woman's car, a blue sedan, about twenty miles outside of town. It was near the dunes and left abandoned. According to the police officer on the scene, the engine was still running and all four doors and the trunk were left open.

Peter, now on his knees in front of the screen moving in closer to make out the face of the woman missing. He covered his face in disbelief. He knew this person. The memory came rushing back and he recognized her beyond a shadow of a doubt. He remembered driving past Kate and this woman on Briggs Way just down the street from their house. They were running together, talking, laughing and taking turns holding Bentley's leash as he ran alongside them.

He slowed down long enough to catch a glimpse of each of them, exchanged waves, and then he kept on driving.

She had been on her way to see him today at the coffeehouse, which means he was the last person to talk with her before she was—he would have to assume—abducted and maybe killed by the same person that killed his wife, the Oceanside Strangler.

CHAPTER SEVEN

Peter exhausted the internet for several more hours while keeping a watchful eye on the time so he wouldn't overlook his three o'clock appointment at the police station.

He searched all avenues for this Murphy character, scrolling through pages of likely choices. Nonetheless, he could come up with nothing that fit the description of the man that darkened his doorway early this morning and pissed off his dog.

Peter then called the Pleasant Bay Sheriff's Office and asked for a Detective Murphy. The desk sergeant that answered the phone acted dumbfounded for a few seconds and then gave his response. "Well, ain't that a head scratcher as there's no one by that name that works here at this precinct. Sorry, man, have a good day."

His suspicions proved to be true now, realizing that anyone can slap a name on a business card, flash a fake badge and make it seem believable.

Detective Elliott or "Big Jake" as he preferred to be called, had guaranteed him that his partner would be able to nail this guy's identity with a few short pencil strokes. It would be hard to believe that anyone could get more than one or two facial features from his pathetic description.

He shut down the computer and then picked up Bentley's collar. With a few more twists and pulls the ribbon and key that once were intertwined were now free. He held it up in front of his face and studied it for a while. The yellow grosgrain ribbon was discolored and the ends were frayed. The key was scratched and tarnished. By the looks of it, the collar had been dragged through the muck and then some. Who knew where Bentley had been all this time and how the ribbon key ended up around his collar.

He sank down into the sofa cushions clutching close to his chest the ribbon key, the one thing that he felt connected to since Kate's tragic death. He was more than confident that it was not going to stay in his hands for long, as now he had no choice but to turn it over to Big Jake, as it was considered evidence and could be useful in finding her killer.

A young sergeant greeted Peter Foster at the front desk at the Chatham Sheriff's Department. Oddly enough he was the only one in the place at this late afternoon hour. He stood at the desk and stared at the sergeant as he shuffled papers into a file cabinet.

This guy had a personality of a toad and did an excellent job of avoiding eye contact by doing nonsense filing while his only customer "so to speak" was staring him down. It seemed as though he was suffering from a painful chip on his shoulder for being stuck with desk duty, nonetheless, he was only speculating.

Feeling his stares, the sergeant slammed the file cabinet drawer hard in frustration and then managed to look up from his monotonous duties long enough to utter three words in Peter's direction, "Come with me."

"Great!" Peter said. "My queue at last," he mumbled under his breath.

The sergeant led him down a narrow hallway and opened the door to a small room adjacent to several offices, all of which were occupied with officers in blue. The sergeant had not planned on keeping him company for any length of time, so grabbing the door knob, he instructed Peter to wait here for Big Jake, then quickly pulled the door shut.

It would be obvious to anyone that the room in which he was placed was designated for interrogating suspects—disconcerting to say the least, as he didn't feel he was a suspect in his wife's murder. Perhaps they were holding out on him and they knew something he did not.

The room to which the sergeant at the front desk with the sunshine and roses personality escorted him was dim and windowless, with concrete gray as its color palate. Dull gray paint was schlepped on the walls from ceiling to floor. An industrial steel table in the center of the cell had two folding chairs tucked underneath that didn't look too convincing that they would hold anyone over a hundred pounds. He chose to stand.

He noticed right away that there wasn't any hardware on this side of the door, so once inside, you were inside to stay until told otherwise.

On the wall was a phone that was also painted in the same dull gray paint. Obviously, the painter was too lazy to remove the phone, so he carelessly painted right over it, not giving it a second thought.

Peter found himself pacing the floor and fidgeting with his hands, growing more impatient with each passing moment. He checked and then re-checked his top pocket to reassure himself that the ribbon key was still there, secure and sealed in a plastic freezer bag.

He could hear someone moving around on the other side of the door and soon to his relief, it opened. Big Jake popped his head inside the room and spewed out a few choice words.

"What the hell! Why did that little weasel at the front desk make you wait in the gray room? Wait. Don't answer that question, as I know the answer. He is downright pissed, that's all. I suppose that's what you get for not following police procedure, but that's another story I won't bore you with. Let's go to my office where it is a bit more civilized. I have a window to the fresh air outside and family photos of my loved ones on my desk."

With a sigh of relief, Peter made a beeline out the door of the so-called gray room and followed the detective to his office at the end of the hallway. He took a seat in a sturdy comfortable chair and welcomed the view out of the window, regardless if it was a parking garage.

He observed Big Jake as he took a seat behind his chaotic desk piled high with stacks of file folders, candy bar wrappers, sticky notes, and a coffee cup with a cartoon character of Dick Tracy talking into his watch. There weren't any photos of family that he could see unless they were buried somewhere under all the crap.

Big Jake had that end-of-the-day look about him and a considerably large stain on the front of his shirt, clear evidence he had spaghetti for lunch. He couldn't help but wonder if he was this disorganized and disheveled, how and the hell would he be able to solve his wife's murder?

There was somewhat of an awkward silence between them as Big Jake scrolled through his emails on his computer, hunting and pecking on the keys with his two index fingers— it was somewhat sad and pathetic to watch. They seemed to be biding time while they waited for his partner to join them. However, it felt like it was the right time to hand over the ribbon key to the detective. He pulled the freezer bag out of his top pocket, first laid it down on the desk, and then slid it across the desk, hesitant to let it go. Big Jake never diverted his eyes from the computer, but made his detective assumption without missing a beat.

"Tell me that is not evidence tucked inside that sealed freezer bag, Mr. Foster?"

"I am afraid it could be, detective. And this is why I am handing it over to you."

"We can only hope there is more than just your fingerprints smeared all over this alleged evidence you have been withholding for how many weeks now, Mr. Foster."

Big Jake picked up the freezer bag and shook his head in disappointment and then set it to the side. He folded his hands and then stared at the man across from him, essentially speechless.

Peter decided to ask a nonsense question to move past this uncomfortable moment.

"How long have you and your partner been partners?"

The detective let out a cleansing breath as he swiveled in his oversized desk chair and then spilled his thoughts out onto the table.

"I would say it's been about six years now, give or take a few months. And you know, I have to tell you that my partner, Grace Harper, may be five foot nothing, but I have witnessed with my own eyes her take down a few punks in an alleyway and make each of them kiss the concrete all without backup, mind you. It was the damnedest thing. You would think she was a detective by day and a super hero by night."

He leaned back in his chair and let out a belly laugh, as if he were the man in the red suit.

There was a light tap on the door and then it was pushed open.

"Well, speak of the devil."

Detective Harper stepped inside the room and closed the door behind her. Clutched in her hands and pressed up against her white tailored shirt was a pad of paper with a sharpened pencil tucked behind her ear. Peter immediately rose to his feet.

"Peter Foster, may I introduce, literally in this case, my partner in crime, Grace Harper."

They extended hands, shook, and then she took the seat next to his.

She was dressed in plain street clothes and masculine shoes. Her strawberry blonde hair was swept back and pulled up into a high ponytail and off her clean makeup-free face.

She was nothing like he envisioned her to be. She wasn't glamorous as they portray female police detectives on the television shows with the big hair and four-inch heels. She was there to do her job, not read a script. She opened up her sketch pad and placed her pencil in her hand.

"When you are ready, Mr. Foster."

CHAPTER EIGHT

The young woman somehow managed to get separated from her girlfriends on the crowded beach, so decided to hail a cab to take her back to the motel to get ready for dinner. She was certain they would already be there and, if not, she could get a head start on showering, hair, and makeup. Fighting over one bathroom with three divas is more than she can handle after a long day in the sun.

She opened the cab door and first tossed her beach bag on the seat, the contents spilling out onto the floorboards. Realizing this, she climbed into the cab spewing out a few swear words and then barked out the name of the motel to the driver. He nodded in her direction and then acknowledged her demand with a, "No problem, miss," however, she wasn't paying any attention. At this point she was bent over and rummaging around for her lipstick and sunblock on the disgusting floorboards of this taxicab. Once she came up for air, feeling a bit pissed off, she wasn't too shy to let him know just how dirty this cab was in her opinion.

"You know I am from New York and I have seen some disgusting taxicabs, but I think this one is by far the worst I have ever been in—I mean ever."

He had no comment to her snide remark, just gripped the steering wheel a little tighter and gritted his teeth. This was his way of keeping his composure and reminding himself to stick to the list. She didn't meet his criteria, yet he felt compelled to make an exception. She could be the exception to the rule, the one off the list.

She took notice that there wasn't the typical partition separating the driver and the passenger—not like back in New York, where all transactions happened through a tiny opening in the heavy plastic. A bobble-head Hawaiian dancer bounced above the meter and a faded used-to-be bumper sticker stuck to the sun-cracked dashboard that displayed the name of the taxi company and slogan, "Cape Cod Cruiser—we will cruise you to anywhere on land."

She rolled her eyes at the corny, yet catchy slogan, and thought to herself she will most likely never forget.

She could only see the back of the driver's head and part of his profile. Even though he was wearing a dark pair of sunglasses, she could feel his eyes penetrating through them somehow in the rear view mirror at her bathing suit top. With a subtle move, she covered herself up. His head turned, diverting back to the road in a matter of seconds.

"Damn it," she blurted out loud. Panicked, she rifled through her beach bag, realizing she didn't have any cash or even her wallet for that matter. She could see the cheesy sign of her motel approaching, as it was flashing the daily rates in red lettering of all colors. This crappy motel was all they could afford, but it didn't much matter, because her and her girlfriends were in Cape Cod for the sun, sand, and partying—not the accommodations.

"Excuse me, I feel horrible, but if you don't mind pulling up to the motel and then waiting for me. I just need to run up to my room and get some cash for you. I promise it will take just a few minutes. I am truly sorry for the inconvenience."

"No problem, miss, however, I will be keeping the meter running and I will not be able to stay in front of the motel. You can find me in the alleyway. I will be waiting there for you."

He dropped her off in front like she asked and then slithered the ole beat-up Pontiac into the alleyway between the motel and what appeared to be a Chinese restaurant. He slid the lever to off-duty, slouched down in his seat, and waited.

CHAPTER NINE

Peter was left alone in Big Jake's office, still sitting in the comfortable chair staring out the window with the so-called view, but not feeling so comfortable at this point.

The detectives that he had come to know were called out to the field and left in a hurry, leaving him alone once again. The little weasel from the front desk had poked his head inside the room, bringing their meeting to an unexpected end. He announced to the detectives that they had found another body, this time down at the Chatham Pier. A twist to this case to say the least, as the last three bodies were found on the beach. Why the change of location? It seemed odd and out of character for this murderer, now a serial killer.

The detective's sketch pad was lying face down literally on the desk and Peter didn't hesitate to pick it up to take a look. He flipped it over and stared down at the pencil sketch transformed into this person in question, Ben Murphy. Maybe a suspect, maybe not, nonetheless, a lead in this case. He would have to give kudos to Detective Harper, as she nailed this guy to a tee.

He quickly snapped a photo of the sketch with his cell phone and then placed the pad back on the desk and then he too made a quick exit.

His logic told him to head for home, but his heart and restless nature sent him straight to the pier. It was just off Shore Road and near his house, so it seemed like the obvious choice to make a detour. He wanted to set his eyes on this team of supposed experts while they were in action and witness just how they handled a crime scene.

He didn't realize just how much time had slipped by since he had been stuck inside the police station, as sunset was in process and going down fast. Feeling frustrated at this entire situation, he yanked the visor down in front of his eyes to block the blinding sunrays obscuring his view of the road. This déjà vu moment sent him back to thinking about his beloved wife, Kate, and how she wished the sun had an on/off switch for these inconvenient times. Her pure innocence and sense of humor he missed so much. What a waste, he thought to himself, of such a beautiful person—*his* person.

He pulled his SUV into the only available space, as all others were taken up by police cars and forensic vehicles. It was his hope to stay under the radar, blend in with the officers, and not get caught nosing around.

He stepped out of his vehicle and slid on his faded blue baseball cap, pulled it down low over his eyes, and made his way toward the fishing pier. There was a group of onlookers huddled together at the edge, obviously abiding by the rules of the bright-yellow crime scene tape and not crossing the line. Peter had no problem excusing himself past the group, ducked under the tape, and headed toward the scene. He wasn't a rule follower, at least not anymore. He heard their whispers, but paid no attention and just kept walking.

Peter could see the body lying there on the pier like a large pile of dead fish. Seagulls hovered above squawking at each other and waiting for their moment to swoop in on the situation. He did his best to divert his eyes from looking or, more likely, staring at the body and busied himself by reading the christened names of the docked sailboats and then looking down at the choppy sea water through the wide cracks of the rickety pier. His stomach was in knots, as he suspects who it might be and, if true, it might overwhelm him.

He moved in as close as he could to watch and listen to the conversations. It seemed that Big Jake's voice carried far and wide.

Big Jake stood over the dead body, his arms crossed in front of him, belly protruding, and feet spread apart. He spewed off at rapid fire some questions to the forensics investigator who was assessing the body.

Forensics investigator and photographer, Parker, didn't have to look up to see who was asking the questions, as he recognized the detective's shoes right off the bat.

"Big Jake, it's nice to see you—I mean smell your shoes. Seriously, you make a nice chunk of change from the department, can't you at least splurge on a new pair of shoes?"

"Hey, stop giving me crap about these shoes. I happen to like them as they suit me and are comfortable. Bought them on eBay, so someone else broke them in for me."

Parker looked up at the detective and said, "So, you are literally walking in someone else's shoes? What the hell is wrong with you?"

He could hear the chuckles from the other officers standing around; Parker looking proud of himself that he came up with the clever joke.

"Okay, let's move on as we are losing daylight," Big Jake grumbled, "What can you tell me about our Jane Doe?"

"White female, approximately 25 to 30 years old. She doesn't appear to have any identification on her person and has been dead anywhere from 24 to 48 hours, however, it is difficult to tell as she has been in the water. I am speculating, but it doesn't appear that she drowned. She was strangled by some sort of leather strap or belt. If you look at her throat you can see the impression of a buckle.

Parker pointed to her throat with his gloved hand and Peter, caught off guard, gasped in horror at the looks of it, but loud enough for everyone to turn around to see who made the noise. Big Jake took a double-take at Peter, and then gave his full attention back to the body.

Parker continued, "It's obvious she was strangled and then tossed into the sea for shark bait. The distraught fisherman you see standing over there next to his boat that he cleverly named 'The Dickens' found her sloshing up against it, tangled in fishing net and crap from the sea."

"Why do you say he cleverly named his boat *The Dickens*, Parker?"

"Charles Dickens was a classic writer, one of my favorites. Don't you read, detective?" Parker responded with judgment in his tone.

"And you're worried about me and my shoes?"

CHAPTER TEN

By the time Big Jake reached the parking lot, Peter Foster was already in his car and backing up. He waved him down, and when that didn't work, he slammed the palm of his hand on the side of his car, which no doubt scared him to a sudden stop. Then Jake knocked on his driver's side window signaling him to stop and roll it down.

"You know, Mr. Foster, it seems that we have a slight problem here. The last time I saw you, you were sitting in my office and now here you are snooping around my homicide investigation. Can you explain yourself or should I have one of the blues take you back to the station and into the gray room and ask you a few necessary questions? I can remember how much you enjoyed sitting in there, but it's your call."

"Look, detective, I came out here because I had my suspicions of who the dead girl might be. And to my relief, and with all due respect to the Jane Doe out there on that dock, it wasn't her. And—it is my understanding that I was not chained to your desk or under arrest, but free to go at any time—isn't that right, detective?" He didn't wait for a response, but continued his rant.

"The woman I expected to see lying under that tarp with the freaking morbid birds circling above her head was the woman that has been missing for some 24 hours now. It was on the news earlier today that they found her car out at the dunes, left abandoned with no sign of the driver anywhere. The owner of that vehicle is now among the missing. They said her name is Kerry Ann—Kerry Ann Hoffman."

"What about her?" The detective leaned both arms down on the window to listen intently. "It sounds like you know more than you are letting on—is this true, Mr. Foster?"

Peter was holding on tightly to the steering wheel and looked away for a split-second, avoiding eye contact altogether. It was apparent that the detective made him nervous to the point of hand sweats and floundering to find his words. And suddenly, to his own surprise, he spilled his guts. He turned his head toward the detective—he was so close he could smell his lunch on his breath. If he had to guess, onions were on the menu.

"I was supposed to meet her at the coffeehouse today when you stopped in for our little chat, but she never showed up, so I brushed it off and went home. She said she had something to tell me and she needed to share something with me about my wife face-to-face. The two of them were friends and did their morning run together."

"You mean to tell me that you were going to meet the woman that was just reported missing less than 24 hours ago?" The detective stared straight into his eyes and shook his head in disbelief while drumming his chunky stout fingers on the car door, his way of showing his impatience and frustration.

However, Peter found himself feeling guilty by association, so he scrambled to tell what he knew. With his hands trembling and a voice now shaky, he did his best to continue with what he remembered.

"Look, I get it. And now that I have had time to put more thought into it, I feel horrible that I didn't report this rendezvous at the coffee house to the authorities. It is obvious now that nobody around here either realizes she is missing or knows her very well."

"Did you know her well, Mr. Foster?" Grace interjected, standing to the side of Jake, moving in closer to the vehicle.

"What? No. God, no! I just told you that she was a friend of my late wife's and I had only seen her once from a distance. She was a runner like my wife, and they were friends, but new friends or acquaintances you might say."

"Well, which is it, friends or acquaintances?" Grace snapped.

"Friends. Yes, they were friends. And if you don't mind, detective, I would like to continue telling you both what I know. Peter took his hat off, so he could see the two detectives better through the window, as now it was pitch dark outside.

"As I was saying, after I came to the station to meet with you, Ms. Hoffman's photo came up on the news that she was missing and my speculation sent me here to the pier, thinking all along it had to be her out there under that tarp."

"When was the last time you communicated with Ms. Hoffman?"

"She first called me to set up the meeting at the coffeehouse. And then I texted her a few times asking where she was and if she was coming at all, but she never responded. And again, that is when you walked in, detective."

"We appreciate your concern, Mr. Foster, however, we can take it from here. I suggest that you get on home and let the experts do the investigating. Sit tight until you hear from us when it comes to your wife's case, and let us find Ms. Hoffman. Is that clear or do you need me to write that down for you?"

"It's clear, detective. It's clear."

Big Jake tapped the top of his SUV twice giving him the go ahead to drive away and leave the scene. Peter shook his head and rolled up the window. He drove off feeling foolish for coming down in the first place.

Grace folded her arms over her chest and together they watched Mr. Foster's tail lights drive out of the parking lot. Jake recognized his partner's expression and knew exactly what she was thinking.

"Go ahead, say what's on your mind, Grace."

"You know, I swear there is more to this guy than we are seeing from the outside. He is hiding something—I can feel it."

CHAPTER ELEVEN

Kerry Ann always assumed that she would live to be an old woman well into her nineties as longevity and good genes were in her favor when it came to her family lifespan. Her grandma lived to be 98 and through her mother's stories she told and re-told about her grandma who lived to be almost a century always created a burst of laughter between her and her sister.

Her mother would say more than often that Grandma was too ornery to die and her ultimate purpose in her long life was to stay here on this earth and punish her loved ones with her orneriness. Plus, she added, God wasn't quite ready for her yet and for God to not have the patience with a little ole lady was definitely saying something.

To think of her mortality now at 54 years old was beyond surreal and something she was not quite ready to face—not yet, not today. She had every intention of getting the hell out of here and was still baffled that her abductor didn't kill her on the spot. What would he want from her and why would he prolong her murder? She was positive he was the Oceanside Strangler and the psycho that killed Kate and the other victims.

He had dragged her flailing body inside this rancid place and across the hard wood-planked floors. He held her wrists together with his gloved hands seemingly concerned and aware of her blindfold, checking it a few times to make certain it stayed intact. It seemed that timing was everything to him and to be the most effective and efficient with his responsibilities to kill and get the job done. She knew in her gut if he had to blindfold her and still had the intentions of killing her in the end, he was an outward coward in her mind and she knew he didn't have the guts to look into the eyes of his next victim.

He moved her swiftly across the floor counting his steps out loud in fives over and over again, 1,2,3,4,5—1,2,3,4,5. His haunting whispers resonated in her mind of how he kept repeating out loud to himself or perhaps for her to witness that he was the Responsible One. He needed to fulfill an agenda and it was crucial to stay on point.

"I cannot disappoint the news media," he said. "I have to uphold my flawless reputation and carry out these murders, so I don't disappoint the viewers. We can't have that can we, Kerry Ann?" He had whispered those frightening words in her ear and his hot disgusting breath penetrating onto her now wet, sweaty, and clammy skin.

He pushed her onto the ground, her final destination in his mind, her whereabouts still undetermined. She leaned against a hard object while he secured her feet together and then her wrists, leaving her hands free. He had one more thing to add.

"It's time for me to go to work, and because of you, there is a possibility I could be late. I hate when people are late. And

I wouldn't want to tarnish my good-standing reputation in this town as a business owner, as that would be irresponsible on my part. I will be back to finish with you, so don't plan on going anywhere, because I will find you no matter what. There is no escape for you, Kerry Ann. You are mine and you are next."

CHAPTER TWELVE

The detectives along with all officers involved with the Oceanside Strangler case dragged themselves into the precinct before sunup and the essential caffeine had a chance to flow through their bloodstreams. They had no choice in the matter, as Big Jake barked out his orders the night before while on the pier and threatened to have them fired if they didn't show up. An empty threat most likely, nevertheless, they weren't taking any chances.

Big Jake made his entrance into the crowded debriefing room still in his rumpled clothes from the night before and headed straight to the suspect board in the front of the room. He set his coffee mug down on the desk and although the idea was futile, he made a reasonable effort to tuck his shirt into his beltless pants.

Detective Harper was sitting in the front row jotting down some last-minute notes on a legal pad, looking somewhat irritated at her partner. She was ready to present her findings pertaining to this case and get the hell out of here so she can do her job. A complete opposite of her partner. And in her own mind, she was prepared, rested, and spotless.

"What did you do—sleep here last night, detective?" one of the officers spewed from the back of the room, creating an outburst of nervous laughter. He deeply regretted the moment the words slipped off his tongue.

Detective Harper turned around in her chair, looking back at the officer, rolled her eyes in his direction, and then turned around once again in time to get a glimpse of her partner's irritated expression.

"Oh crap, this isn't going to go well," she mumbled under her breath.

Big Jake paced back and forth shaking his head and smirking at the officer toward the back of the room.

"Thank you for your mockery, Officer Bradley, is it? I have to say at this hour of the morning, it's greatly appreciated. And, to answer your smart-ass question, yes, I did stay here last night, but didn't sleep, which is what most of you slackers were doing instead of helping my partner and me on this case. So, if you're finished with the sarcastic remarks, I need all of you to listen up—enough chatter and let's get to it."

He flipped over the white board and took a seat on the corner of the desk, folded his arms over his stained, wrinkled shirt and stood, feet apart, stomach spilling out over the top of his pants. Not a pretty sight. However, those that were staring had no choice in the matter.

"As you can see from the sparse white board behind me, we are lacking in suspects to investigate. It is obvious that our main goal is to protect the safety of the people of Chatham and assure them we have some leads. I am certain you heard by now that the news media has dubbed the killer, the Oceanside

Strangler, and rightly so. And now after four murders and one person missing, he is considered a serial killer. His method of killing his victims is to strangle the life out of them and leave their cold lifeless bodies in a wide-open space for the frightened residents of this small town to discover. His choice of weapon is not the typical knife, gun, or anything that would leave a mess behind or a trail of evidence or even fingerprints for that matter. He uses whatever is on their person, whether it's a purse strap, belt, or scarf. Other than the unidentified victim we found at the pier last night, the beach is his choice of drop off. Somehow, the young girl on the pier doesn't seem to fit his pattern, nevertheless, she was strangled like the others."

Big Jake glanced over at his partner for a brief moment, realizing by the annoyed look on her face it was time to give her the floor. One simple nod in her direction, she was up and on her feet with the grace and dignity that exemplified her good name. Detective Grace Harper turned to the officers in the room and dug in her heels in a firm confident stance on the dingy white linoleum floor.

"First of all, let me begin by saying that my partner seems to be dead set on believing that the psychopath out there who is killing these innocent women is a male. On the other hand, there has been no evidence to suggest that is the case, so I wanted to clarify that up front. The odds are high that this person in question is male, but let's not be hasty with the facts. No offense, Jake, just saying what's on my mind." Grace gave a nod to her partner, which he ignored, so she continued her briefing.

"As you can see, behind me is a sketch of this Ben Murphy

character described by Mr. Foster, the first victim's husband. For some odd reason, he showed up on his doorstep giving him some line of crap that he was on this case, flashed some bogus police badge, and filled his head with what anyone on the street could get off any news broadcast. His real name is Dave Murphy, a disgruntled county employee wishing and hoping for that gold watch and a retirement plan. He ended up getting fired for disorderly conduct. I have nothing further to report, other than he is staring at four walls in the county jail for impersonating an officer of the law. He is off the streets and that's a good thing. If anyone in this room would like to volunteer and continue to investigate him, please take care of it. For now, he stays on the suspect board, behind bars, and off my excruciating, long, and agonizing list."

"The person we need to be most concerned about at this time is the woman that has been missing, Kerry Ann Hoffman. She is a resident and business owner here in Chatham and is in her early fifties. According to Peter Foster, his deceased wife Kate and Kerry Ann were friends and spent a great deal of time together. She has a sister that lives a few hours from here and we have yet to be able to reach her by phone or email. Her name is Wendy Hill and I expect she is going to want answers to many questions as to her sister's whereabouts when the time comes. Kerry Ann's car was found out at the dunes, engine running, and all doors including the trunk left open, but seemingly not a bit of evidence to be found.

"In my experience, every killer has a momentary lapse in judgment and fails to pay attention to the smallest of details. Something might slip through their fingers literally and he or she may fail miserably to check or take notice as they walk away from a scene of their heinous crime. Maybe, just maybe, they hesitate for a split second to turn around and check the scene one more time, just once more. Nonetheless, they make the incriminating choice to never look back—walk away— conceivably and secretly wishing to be caught. Psychopathic killers always want to be caught. For them, it's human nature to feel the rush, to want the chase and eventually in the end get caught in the act of murder."

Detective Harper reaches between the pages of her legal pad to pull out a sealed package. She holds it up in front of the officers, swinging it back and forth, portraying a bit of arrogance in her attitude, then she leans forward and lowers her voice to a whisper ...

"They should have looked back."

CHAPTER THIRTEEN

K erry Ann had been struggling for what seemed like hours to remove the blindfold he placed securely over her eyes, as that was the last thing he did before he shoved her into the trunk of his car. Given that her wrists and ankles were still bound together with tape, she used the exposed sticky part on her wrists to her advantage to pull down the blindfold far enough to see what sort of hell hole he put her in.

She never realized how much inner strength she had as she kicked, screamed, and tried to scratch any part of his body she could reach. She missed all but once, the feeling satisfying as her fingernails came in contact with his sweaty rugged skin, digging in deep and gliding down his face as if she was moving in slow motion across a chalk board.

He pulled away screaming out in pain, wiping the blood from his wounds. He called her a bitch and then slammed the trunk down hard, locking her inside. A short rough ride, if she had to guess, maybe twenty minutes brought her to this godforsaken place. She couldn't help but wonder whether this was where he had intended to take her or was it just convenient so he wouldn't get caught in the process.

The struggle to see was now over. For what she could make out, she was in an abandoned fishing warehouse and surrounding her and covering the wood-planked floorboards were dead fish carcasses, hundreds of skeleton bones just lying there rotting in their graves, left for dead like her. The stench permeated the air causing her eyes and nostrils to burn and sent her stomach churning.

Above her were broken-down rafters and an unfortunate rat infestation. They seemed to be utilizing it as a balance beam and source of transportation from one side of the warehouse to another.

"It had to be rats," she whispered to herself. "God, how I hate rats."

She sat there for quite some time feeling helpless and vulnerable. Her mouth was dry, and her skin was crawling with even the slightest thought of what he might do to her when he returns from his "so-called" responsibilities. She couldn't even remotely imagine this monster working, owning a business and working among the people of this town and putting on a front, this fake Good Samaritan attitude, while deciding on who his next victim would be, who he would kill next.

She tried to figure out how long she had been here from the moment he took her from the alleyway behind her office, to the trunk of his car to this place. It had to be at least two days, if not more.

She had to assume that someone had to be looking for her by now—maybe Peter Foster, as he was her last contact, even though they were strangers. Hell, he made it clear what he thought of her from the start and she knew he didn't give a shit about her whereabouts or well-being. He most likely didn't think anything was wrong as to why she didn't show up at the coffeehouse. He had to assume that she had forgotten or changed her mind at the last minute. She deeply regretted not telling Peter about the secrets Kate had kept from him and shared with her for those several weeks she was being stalked by the psycho that she was most certain was Kate's killer and now her abductor. Kate made it clear she didn't want anyone to know. It almost seemed as if she liked the attention she was getting from the incessant onset of letters he was leaving in unobtrusive places. Nonetheless, Kate seemed to find them—even go searching for the next one and then the next, as if it was something she found herself looking forward to for some odd reason.

It wasn't until the last letter she received, the one before she went missing—that something wasn't quite right with Kate. Her attitude had shifted drastically, and she refused profusely to discuss the letter or its content and brushed it off as if it were nothing. She did, however, mention this letter, the last letter she found inside the house instead of the mailbox or tucked between the cracks next to the kitchen window. This time, she had found it on her dresser where Peter could have stumbled upon it at any given time. This was shocking to say the least and she could see from the terrified expression on Kate's face there was more to this than she imagined. Now, she wished she would have gone directly to the police, or at least told Peter. Kate made her promise she wouldn't breathe a word, as she didn't want to worry her husband.

Managing to stand up on her feet, she maneuvered herself to the center of the room, noticing two boarded-up windows and a door that blended into the wall, making it look small and insignificant—nevertheless, a possible way out.

Surrounding the perimeter of the building were several broken-down freezers stacked on end, doors off the hinges, all empty of what might have been when this warehouse was up and running. There was one particular freezer that was sitting upright. It was obvious it had been moved away from the others, as the drag marks on the floor looked recent.

A combination lock was threaded through the rusty metal hook dangling loosely, an open invitation to raise the lid and see what was inside. Her gut was wrenching, and her intuitive emotions were in high gear and off the charts of the horrific sight she would witness inside this abandoned box, yet her curiosity drew her in.

She squeezed her eyes shut as the haunting images flashed in her mind of what her dear friend Kate might have looked like when they found her dead lifeless body lying on the beach.

Kerry Ann's wrists still bound with tape, yet her fingers were free, so she lifted the lid and pushed it up and over, where it slams hard on the other side. The silence in the air is now interrupted by her horrific screams and sheer panic. She stared down at the cold dead body of a young woman looking her up and then down again as she saw gripped between her black and blue fingers was the killer's calling card, his signature of sorts and damn proud of it. May I introduce you to Responsible Number, 1,2,3,4,5 ... Responsible Number Five.

CHAPTER FOURTEEN

H e pulled into the gas station, bypassing the pumps altogether and drove straight to the self-serve carwash. It was somewhat hidden from the main road and would give him ample time to think things through and wash whatever he thought needed to be washed off his cab, inside and out. His shift was about to start, and he had less than twenty minutes to get it done and clock in on time.

It was a two-fold situation when it came to his job and his boss didn't tolerate any cabbie being late coming or going, and God forbid if there was a speck of dirt anywhere to be found on the cabs when they rolled into the lot. The standards of this company were high, and he needed this job in more ways than one and did his best to abide. His boss's motto was clear and concise, if the cabs were returned dirty then they stayed on the lot and the driver took a walk—simple as that.

The annoying voice he so despised screeched over the radio, interrupting his thoughts and at last in time while hosing down his cab as instructed. The voice on the other end of the cheap radio was pleading for an ETA from Cabbie 47. He apparently was assigned the title Cabbie 47, according to the paperwork and ugly profile picture of himself slapped up on the dashboard for all to see. He never had the pleasure of meeting that annoying voice that called out to him and the others. Nonetheless, if he did, he would most likely punch him in the nose just for sake of being annoying. His voice sounded weak and submissive and he hated that—no, despised it. He answered regardless, turning on his pleasantries in fear of losing this job altogether. After all, he had a family to feed.

"Yes, this is Cabbie 47. What do you want? I am on my way back to the lot. Give me ten minutes—okay? I am not going to be late, I promise."

"I need you to go to PC."

"What's PC? I haven't worked for this company long enough to know what PC means, sorry."

"Go to the private channel. Trust me," the annoying voice insisted.

He sat up a little taller, switched to the private channel, and rested his elbows on the steering wheel, intrigued and ready to hear the urgent message.

"Are you there?" he said, unsure if he had the right connection.

"Did you pick up a fare from the beach the other day and drop her off at a motel?"

"I pick up fares all day long from the beach, so how am I supposed to remember, especially being it was two days ago. That would be a stretch of my memory to say the least. I can barely remember this morning, let alone forty-eight hours.

"I never mentioned it was two days ago—I said the other day. You added the two days. So let me ask you once again.

Did you pick up a fare on the beach around 6:30, and yes, two days ago—a young woman, very attractive, riding solo, said to be in her mid-twenties. The cabbie dropped her just a few short blocks up the strip at the low budget motel—you know, the one on Fifth?"

He paused for a few seconds and tried to jog his memory of this woman in question and answered the annoying voice with a confident response.

"It doesn't ring a bell with me, and I don't appreciate the third degree."

"Look, you better get here fast—the entire police force is on the premises searching every vehicle for any trace of evidence left behind by this woman. And there's this relentless detective that I am pretty sure he thinks he's Colombo asking way too many questions."

"Why would they need to be looking for evidence of this woman?"

"Because she's dead."

CHAPTER FIFTEEN

Peter was allowing the guilt to eat at him for the many reasons that were out of his control. With Kate dead, Kerry Ann missing, and this psychotic killer terrorizing this small town, he couldn't help but think there had to be something he was missing in this investigation. Not that he claimed this investigation to be his own, nonetheless, it was his wife, his loss, and in his mind, now his responsibility. He planned to trace his steps back to before Kate was killed to see if there was a small piece of the puzzle he could fit into this big gap of frustration.

He had already been warned numerous times by the detectives to back off and let them do their job, yet his emotions were far too deep to abide by their adamant requests at this point in time. There wasn't anything that would or could stand in his way of getting justice for his wife's murder.

He stood at the kitchen window mesmerized by the ominous clouds rolling in and listened to the thunder rumbling in the distance. To him, it was comforting, but to Bentley, the frightening sound sent him shivering and shaking to his feet every time. He knew it would be a matter of seconds before he made a beeline for the kitchen searching for his protector, his defender of all thunderstorms. Not to disappoint, he made his way around the corner and landed his eighty-pound pile of mush at his feet for safety.

Peter's thoughts and memories were focused on his beloved Kate, as he watched the steady rain come down off the roof and puddle onto the sidewalk. He recalled making a mental note to clean out the gutters, but somehow that didn't seem relevant anymore—what difference would it make now? This house means nothing to him without her in it, and he planned on putting it up for sale as soon as possible. He could still see her out of the corner of his eye at times walking the hallways, not as a ghostly presence, but as if she had left a permanent stain in this house and she was still here somehow, comforting him through this incredible terrifying nightmare.

He swore he could feel her leaning up against him at the kitchen window and caressing his arm like she had for so many years. She had such a light touch that would send excitement through his body and goose bumps rising up on his skin. He never grew tired of her touch, her smile, her laughter. He never took her for granted for one second of their long marriage. And as far as he knew, they told each other everything. They had no secrets between them—not one.

The house phone rang, startling Peter out of his trance and back to the reality of what was next. He answered with his normal introduction, "This is Peter Foster," in his monotone mundane voice. On the other end, the man simply breezed past his own introduction, wasting no time to address the topic at hand. This lack of giving his name was frustrating to say the least to Peter, as he didn't tolerate ill-mannered people very well. They pissed him off and theoretically put him over the proverbial edge that he was already hanging onto for dear life.

"Hold on, hold on. Wait a minute. Do you have a name, young man? I think it's only proper if I have given mine, you can be polite enough and give me yours. It's effortless really and will only take a second."

"My deepest apologies, Mr. Foster, please allow me to start over. My name is Parker and I am a forensic photo investigator for the Chatham Police Department, and I have been assigned to your late wife's case. You have already been introduced to the other primary detectives on this case, Detectives Elliot, and Grace Harper. I am calling today, because I have some information regarding the evidence that you presented to Detective Elliott—you might recall it being the ribbon with the key attached to it or perhaps I should say keys."

"What do you mean keys, detective? I know there was a house key attached to that ribbon and never noticed another key. I am sorry, I am not understanding the relevance. However, I would like to know if you have a suspect yet?"

"Let's just say we have someone of interest, although there have been no arrests. I can assure you, Mr. Foster, if we did, you would be the first to know. The entire department is working 24/7 to find evidence that could prosecute this person and we are not stopping there. I would like to add that we cannot give credit to the ribbon key for this person of interest I have mentioned to you. Nevertheless, I have found something that could lead us down another path."

Peter sat down at the kitchen table and let out a sigh.

"I'm listening. Go on."

"Mr. Foster, I realize the large key is the house key. But looped through the ribbon and wedged between the double knot was a smaller key, sort of old-fashioned, pewter in color, and definitely not a match to your house—more like a key to a safe or one of those old metal cash boxes from back in the day."

"I wasn't aware there was another key tied to that ribbon. My wife … ," he said, but his voice trailed off as he struggled to choke back the tears. He managed to clear his throat, compose himself and continue with his story. "My wife made it a habit of hanging that ribbon with the key on the end of it on a hook along with my dog's leash outside the mudroom after her daily run. I never looked at it close enough, nor did I want to take a closer look at it. Even when I was attempting to untangle it from my dog's collar I didn't notice this key you speak about. It seems my eyes are worse off than I thought, detective."

"I will text you a photo of the key, Mr. Foster. And if you could search your house and your wife's belongings, perhaps we could find what it opened and then we can move forward. There hasn't been much evidence presented, though my gut is telling me that this key just might lead us down another path, and we can hope that it won't be a dead end."

Peter stood at the doorway to Kate's walk-in closet and stared into the darkness, trying his best to talk himself into stepping inside. It would require just two steps on his part and a quick tug on the string that was attached to the 60-watt light bulb that would shed some light on his wife's personal belongings she had no choice but to leave behind.

He recalled her nagging him on the many occasions to install the "proper lighting," she called it, and of course he would grumble his answer that he would eventually get around to it. She knew what that meant.

He wasn't sure why he felt compelled to look at her things and what the hell he would be searching for other than this metal box the forensic investigator conjured up in his mind that would accommodate an oddly shaped key. He took a look at the image on his phone this Detective Parker texted to him once more before he started rifling through her things. He felt guilty doubting Kate's honesty after all these years. What would she be hiding in this dimly lit closet?

He felt uncomfortable looking through her private things without Kate here to orchestrate this activity. She would move him aside for fear of him messing up this method to her OCD madness and take over the search.

He pulled one box down after another and shuffled through its contents, all while wiping the tears away. It was painful to go back and look at the many photos of their life together. It was always just the two of them standing in front of museums, beachfronts, and amazing romantic sunsets. She saved everything from their trips from airline stubs, receipts, and napkins from the restaurants they patronized, swearing to him she would put them all in an album one day. Now that one day would never come.

He stacked one box on top of one another and noticed something sticking out from under one of them. It was a letter that had been taped to the bottom of the color-coded box for their trip to Colorado last winter.

He held the pale gray envelope in his hands and stared down at the unfamiliar handwriting, his thoughts racing along with his broken heart. It was then that he realized his once steady, strong hands were not so steady anymore. He could see the lined paper through the envelope and its contents felt significant. The envelope wasn't addressed to Mr. and Mrs. Foster, Kate Foster, or even Kate for that matter.

He struggled to focus his tear-filled eyes on what he was reading and found the words to be inconceivable. In his hands he was holding what appeared to be a death threat towards his wife. In his hands he was holding a letter from his wife's killer. He dropped to his knees and read the toxic threatening words out loud as if it were to make it a reality somehow.

To the Perfect One, the one I am responsible for, the one I will kill first, You Kate, will be my Responsible Number One …

CHAPTER SIXTEEN

Cabbie 47 turned down the well-traveled road that led to the cab company and lot. He did his best to dodge the scattered potholes the city hadn't had a chance to repair yet or, more likely, be able to afford to repair. Cash wasn't exactly overflowing in this city during season or off.

It was unfortunate for his clean vehicle that the rain was now pounding his windshield and he was now reluctant to switch on the wipers for fear of making a smeared mess and not passing "the clean" inspection from his boss. He had no choice, as it was coming in from all directions.

He rolled up to the gate where he was greeted by a large-sized police officer, both in height and in width. At least, he assumed he was a police officer by his authoritative demeanor. His uniform was camouflaged by a plastic raincoat doing a piss-poor job of protecting him from the monsoon that was engulfing this town. The officer bent down to his level, and when their eyes met he gave him the one finger signal to roll his window down so he could give him direction on what to do next. The officer was a man of few words, pointed to where he was to park and then stepped back from the vehicle and looked away.

The officer seemed disgusted, and he couldn't blame him. He was soaked to the skin and stuck here being the gatekeeper and not the investigator. Guess it's the way it goes when you pull the short straw.

The cab driver cranked up his window and then wiped the rain spatter off the seal and onto his pants. From the look of this place the entire police force was on the premises. He couldn't help but think if the entire police force was here, then who was policing this small town and keeping the good people safe. After all, there was a serial killer on the loose. He found that somewhat amusing for some reason and laughed right out loud. Why not, nobody was listening.

He followed the orders given by what's his name, officer gatekeeper, and knew it was inevitable he would have to cross through the gates and face not only the badges, but his freaking boss. God, he hated that guy. He could swear he was one of those shady characters that stepped straight out of a comic book. Short, fat, beady eyes, cigar-smoking son-of-a-bitch. There were times he wished he could run him over with his cab and then back up just to make sure those beady eyes were no more.

He pulled into his assigned spot, his headlights blinding the officer that stood in front of him, arms crossed, legs apart. Again wearing that plastic shit they call a raincoat and looking worn-out and haggard. He motioned him to move forward and then held out one hand indicating stop and to stay put.

"What is it with the hand gestures?" he mumbled to

himself. "Must be prerequisite at the police academy, hand gestures 101." He let out a nervous laugh and put his cab into park.

He could feel his body tense up in anticipation of it all. Nervous energy sent him fidgeting with his seatbelt, hesitant to unfasten it or wait. He then moved his personal items around on the front seat only for them to fall back to the same position they were in before.

The police officer pounded his fist on the hood of the cab, which was his cue to get out and let them go ahead with the infamous search. He could sense the officer's intolerance for this entire ordeal in progress and he would be certain to try to not piss him off in any way possible, yet he couldn't promise.

He unfastened his belt, grabbed his stuff on the seat, feeling clumsy and rushed. He attempted to open the door remembering that it would stick a little in inclement weather. It took a few shoves to make it happen.

Feeling somewhat ridiculous as he stepped out onto the wet pavement, the officers stared him down as if he was some hardened criminal. Even though they weren't laughing at him, he could tell they wanted to give him shit about it, just because they could.

"I need you to stand in the front of the cab and stay in the light so I can keep an eye on you," the officer spouted off, giving this simple instruction, but hoping this guy wouldn't give him any shit.

"You are not to move, talk, blink, or take in a deep breath until we are done searching your vehicle. Is that understood?"

"Yes, of course, officer. I would be happy to oblige and

cooperate in any way. I have to say the entire department is doing a remarkable job here today. I commend all of you. Really, I do."

The officer rested his hands on the cab, looked down and shook his head with exasperation before making his strong presence known by standing inches from this smart ass's nose.

"And, if I may add one more thing, whatever your name is, and I honestly don't care at this point, don't freaking patronize me or any of the police officers on this case. Got it? I can't speak for my colleagues, yet that happens to be one of my biggest pet peeves. Trust me, you wouldn't want to clean up the mess from my head exploding all over your cab, would you? How is that for a hypothetical visual, Cabbie 47, is it?"

"No, sir, I am sure that would not be a pleasant sight to see and I will certainly take your word for it. Whatever you say, officer. I just find it easy to compliment the deserving."

From where he stood, he had a clear view of the cab company's office and standing in the entrance was his boss and two cabbies. He recognized them but didn't have a clue what their names were and, in truth, didn't give a shit. His boss's back was to him, yet he could see the nasty smoke from his cigar pooling around him like a storm of soot. He smoked like a chimney and his cancer sticks seemed to be a permanent fixture, his rotten teeth grinding the tip, and then spitting out the remains like a stale piece of gum.

He couldn't hear the conversation of the trio, yet he could see from their demeanor that it was heated. His boss had to be feeling the pressure from the police, as one of his drivers had given this Jane Doe in question, a short ride and then just twenty-four hours later was found dead at the pier. An unfortunate situation for all parties and he simply wanted to get it over with and clear his good name.

The officers put on their gloves, entered the vehicle and started shoving their hands between the seats and gliding along the floorboards blindly, depending on their gloved hands to capture the evidence in question and in search of something, anything in hopes to nail this guy.

Cabbie 47 watched the officers through the windshield sweep his vehicle and place whatever they found inside the heavy coated plastic bag on the passenger seat, the bag was marked evidence with a black marker. The entire process took about 15 minutes and then the verdict.

The officer returned to his position standing inches from the cabbie's nose, looked him square in the eyes, and said,

"For the record, your vehicle has been impounded."

CHAPTER SEVENTEEN

He was prepared to walk away from the two officers that ransacked his vehicle scrutinizing every inch and everything from a candy wrapper to a piece of lint. They did give him the free to go "for now" comment, which motivated him to get the hell out of there in a hurry.

He had convinced himself over and over that he cleaned everything up off the freaking floorboards at the car wash— evidently that wasn't the case. Whatever they found was now in their possession and was enough in their minds to impound his cab. How could he have been so careless, so irresponsible? After all, he had a lot at stake—his job, his family, very little cash in the bank.

He could feel the stares of the officers penetrate through his entire body as he headed toward the chain link fence and gate, his entrance clearly now his exit. The dedicated police officer he had christened, "the gatekeeper," was still doing his due diligence, keeping a watchful eye on those coming and going. He couldn't help but to be relieved for the guy that the rain had finally stopped.

His thoughts were racing in all directions as to the

unanswered questions of what was happening around him—was he fired, was he under investigation? What did the officers find in his cab that would make them feel as though they needed to impound it? He couldn't afford to be out of work, and he needed the wheels to do what he had to do in this small town.

He could feel his body sway back and forth and was starting to lose it. It felt like he was having one of those out of body experiences that he heard about from many people. They described it in great detail, but he had never thought it stood to be true.

He walked these train tracks many times day and night, rain or shine, and never saw a moving train or even heard one in the distance. The farther he walked, the colder it felt and for the first time he could see his warm breath escaping his lungs to blend into the night air. Summer seemed to disappear overnight and a chill was finding its way into this small town with this unexpected cold blast.

He stared down at the tracks taking larger steps than his usual gate would allow, making him lose his balance a few times, but catching himself before he fell straight to the ground and onto the tracks. He would literally kill for a brown paper bag with a bottle of something inside, something strong, as he wasn't going to be too choosy as anything would do to warm him up from the inside out.

Reaching in his pocket he could feel the AA token which was a constant reminder of his three years of sobriety. He knew that the bottle he was wishing for was nothing but a hypothetical and he wasn't about to destroy what he had worked so hard for—that token was an achievement—a backslide was not going to materialize. Something he had to convince himself of every day of his sad pathetic life.

He had taken this path home before on shifts when he had to leave his cab behind. He much preferred driving his cab home and parking it, or rather hiding it, inside his one-car garage so his boss wouldn't do a drive by, as he was known to do on occasion. His cab was his only source of transportation other than his rusty ole bicycle he had since he was 15 years old. It was the bike or bus, but at least he had choices.

His neighborhood was considered small for this town, an obvious on the other side of the tracks housing development, and nothing like the mansions on the beachfront. Sand and surf and the salty breeze are something he would never have in his lifetime. Nonetheless, he worked hard to put food on the table for his family and that is all that mattered.

There were twenty-five houses crammed together in his development. All the houses were painted in the same hideous nonexistent color of concrete slab gray. It was low-income housing, nevertheless, it wasn't so horrible that it wasn't livable for those on a fixed income. It was what he and his wife could afford now that she was expecting their first child in less than six months.

They rented this house on a month-to-month basis from an arrogant SOB who called himself a real estate broker by trade and landlord by night. He would come around checking on the place to make sure they were taking care of it, pointing out stupid shit and threatening to evict them if one blade of grass was longer than the others. He would be there to collect the rent on the first of the month before the sun came up, demanding cash. No checks allowed. He was never late to collect, not once.

The one thing his wife of 15 years loved about their house was the white picket fence that surrounded it. She said it made her feel normal somehow, and safe. He knew he would never be able to give her normal—not ever—not really.

He stopped short from his house as he could see there was an unmarked police car in his cramped driveway. Some of his neighbors were standing outside in their pajamas or so it appeared, drinking a beer and pointing at his house and making assumptions, no doubt. He stepped back and crouched down beside some oversized bushes and a couple of trashcans. If anyone saw him at this point, they would make a presumption that he was guilty of whatever he was guilty of. It couldn't look good from any standpoint.

He had to make some sort of decision to save face from his neighbors' constant scrutiny. They obviously had nothing better to do on a Sunday night, other than shoot the shit about the house behind the normal picket fence. Not so much sunshine and roses, or so it seems.

CHAPTER EIGHTEEN

D etective Grace Harper stood on the corner of Main and Central holding in one hand the missing woman's photo and in the other a cup of coffee. With one cold sip left, she downed it and -tossed the empty cup into the trashcan. Then she slipped the crinkled photo of the missing woman into her top pocket, all while punching the button for the crosswalk.

She was dressed in her "go to" uniform, the typical khaki pants, white starched slim-fit oxford button down, always tucked in and belted, and a lightweight jacket that she had left open more for style than use. Her hair had been freed from her tight ponytail and her blonde curls fell softly over her shoulders. It was a nice change and made her come across more approachable and warmer. Shielding her hazel eyes were her favorite Aviators, a part of her ensemble she would be sure never to leave behind.

Her constant scrutiny of complete strangers was something that she could on no account turn off. It was in her blood always to be the detective and to doubt most people, as most people would look right into your eyes and lie right to your face with no hesitation. She could spot the liars, the storytellers, the guilty as charged in nothing flat, but never let them know she knew. It was a gift and she used it to her advantage.

She needed to find this psycho, the guilty individual that was strangling the innocent women of this small town. He or she was out there and couldn't hide much longer, as they were bound to make a mistake along their gruesome path.

Grace assessed the people roaming the town, all strangers to her, strolling the sidewalks with time on their side and shopping the storefronts that were all lined up in a convenient row. It was apparent they were tourists who seemed willing to spend their hard-earned money on crappy tee shirts with lighthouses stamped on the front and Chatham, Massachusetts in an oversized hideous font on the back. It didn't seem to matter to them that both would inevitably peel off after the first wash and dry.

It was obvious to the police department and detectives that the locals were on edge, yet they seemed to be willing to keep their shops and restaurants opened—business as usual so as to not frighten the tourists away. By now the tourists had seen the front-page news of the murders in this town, but they seemed more concerned with sticking to their rigid vacation schedule they had saved up for all year. They were determined to use and fill every minute of their vacation, regardless of the chaos and danger surrounding them.

Once season was over, his town turned into the notorious ghost town, tourists gone, stores closed, sending the locals hibernating until the weather changed for the good. They had no choice but to make it now, as the winter months were brutal for the store owners' bank accounts.

Most of the locals knew of Kerry Ann's company, yet hadn't had a chance to get to know her personally. From what Grace had found out, Kerry Ann had been in town for just a few months and her only family member she caught wind of back at the station was a sister. She couldn't help but speculate why the sister hadn't arrived yet to partake in the search. Nobody has heard from her since they found Kerry Ann's car at the dunes. Who knows, maybe she was a figment and whoever called the station was another clue to these murders.

The thought of her youngest sister came to mind then, but again she was always in her thoughts and the reason she walked the creaky floorboards of her apartment each and every single grueling sleepless night for the past 18 years. It is without a doubt, the reason why she became an insomniac. Being an insomniac wasn't that bad, as she had learned how to fill those dark irritatingly quiet hours with all sorts of tasks, accomplishing quite a bit, other than sleep. Although the tears have stopped, the flashes of the gruesome discovery in her family home would never fade.

Grace Harper grew up in the windy city along with her five siblings and parents who managed to stay married even though she knew they weren't happy. Her mother, "B," short for Beatrice, was a lovely woman and a good mother to her and her brothers and sisters. She recalled hearing her mother say on many occasions how much she hated—no—despised her name and instructed everyone to call her "B"—just the letter "B", never Bea. She would put on the happy face and smile at her children and friends, although her eyes would tell a much different story. Grace had an intuitive way about her and perhaps her mom did, too, as there were times her and her mother's eyes would meet, and she knew Grace would know what she was really thinking or feeling. Her mother would put on the happy face, but deep down she knew she was sad about so many things.

They lived in a two-story house that was dirt free and cozy and the door was always revolving with the neighborhood kids coming and going. The kitchen eternally smelled like cookies and the counter full of baked goods and candy dishes filled up with assorted chocolates. She could recall her friends asking if they were rich and, of course, that wasn't even in the least bit close to the truth, however, she didn't let them know either way. She overheard her dad on the phone begging the bank to give him an extension on his mortgage payment, not once but many times. She ignored it for the most part, however, it weighed on her mind in the middle night. Too young to do anything about it as she didn't much understand the perimeters of a mortgage, even so she knew her parents were struggling to make ends meet.

That night …

18 years ago, Chicago, Illinois

It was snowing and the temperature was below zero, as usual. She pulled out her key to the front door, however, didn't need to use it as the door was already unlocked and opened just a crack. She pushed on it and it swung open and then bounced back a little letting out its creepy creaking noise everyone grew accustomed to and expected. The house didn't feel right. Something wasn't right.

There wasn't anyone home. And how could that be as there were so many of them—someone was always at home. She could hear music coming from down in the basement, as that is where the laundry room was and the furnace to this old house. Her mother spent so much time down there folding and washing the endless piles of dirty clothes for this family and would turn on the small radio to keep her company.

Grace didn't bother to take off her boots or gloves, she headed straight toward the basement and followed the music. She cautiously made her way in the direction of the music and started down the steep stairs. As she descended the staircase, she held on tightly to the wooden railing. The closer she got to the bottom, she knew from the hairs standing on the back of her neck that what she was about to discover wasn't going to be a good thing.

She sees her sister's shoe, just lying there chaotically on its side at the bottom of the stairs and when she turned the corner, she found her body next to the furnace. She stood over her and stared down at her sister's cold limp lifeless body just lying there—her lips were blue as if someone has squeezed the life and breath out of her. The music on the radio seemed to get louder in her head and the furnace kicked on at the same time, causing her to let out a blood-curdling scream. It didn't sound like anything was coming out of her mouth, as if she were screaming only in her head and not out loud.

She placed both hands over her ears and screamed again as

loud as she could. Nobody could hear her—there was no one around. Her sister's eyes were open staring straight up at the ceiling. She wasn't moving, she wasn't breathing.

"Excuse me. You okay, miss? Your phone is ringing, and you are sort of in everyone's way." Some stranger tapped her on the shoulder and asked her the question, bringing her out of this freak trance she was in while standing in the middle of the sidewalk.

Grace fumbled for her phone inside her pocket and answered it sounding as if she just woke up from a deep sleep. "Yes, this is Detective Harper. What is it?" she said, seemingly irritated with herself.

"Do you know where the old fishing warehouse is off Briggs Way? You better head over there ASAP!" The phone went dead.

CHAPTER NINETEEN

It was time to go back for her. It was time to check her off his list, his Responsible Number Six. It had been too long. He should have killed her on the second day like he did the others, and he despised himself for waiting. She had to have known that it was inevitable that she would die and her only way out of this nightmare regardless, as he would give her no other option.

He needed her to be ready for him—she had no choice. But now he had something to look forward to—he was obsessed with the thought of strangling this one, his weapon of choice this time would be his bare hands. It was time to go back to the warehouse and finish her off before the rats beat him to it.

The beads of sweat began to form on his temple and his heartbeat quickened. He found the thought of going back for her to be exciting, exhilarating. It brought him back to the first one, the first one he was responsible for, the first one on his proverbial list.

The recollection of that day was easy to recall, since she was his first. It was her special day and he made sure that he stayed back a few feet from her doing any and all things possible to blend in with the crowd and becoming just another runner on the beachfront. He had been watching her for weeks and knew her every move and daily routine. It thrilled him to know that there was an inevitable outcome for her, yet she was clueless of his plan. She was more than clueless—she would be dead in less than 48 hours.

Her beauty radiated over the others and he admired her for her tenacity to exercise and stay in shape and to want to take care of herself, especially a woman of her age. He didn't know for sure but if he were to take a stab at it, she might be in her late fifties—early sixties, at least 15 years his senior. Regardless, her body was fit, and it showed.

He was able to get so close to her, so close that he could hear the air in her lungs inhale and exhale. She paid no attention to him. And why would she, as she was focused on the pavement beneath her shoes? Her loyal dog ran alongside her and he didn't find him to be a threat as he looked the part of her workout. He wanted to reach out and touch her face and feel the bone structure of her jaw and softness of her skin on her neck. He could envision wrapping his large sweaty hands around her throat and challenging her to try and swallow. The strength of his hands would be too much for her to bear—he would overcome her in a matter of minutes, and that was a given. He knew it and she would eventually experience it. He wanted to watch her gasp for air and take her last breath while she struggled to convince him with the terrified look in her watery eyes begging him to set her free, pleading for her life, asking for mercy on her poor innocent soul. He got what he wanted. He made it happen. She was dead and now found. He was responsible for her death. He was the Responsible One to kill her—after all, it was her time to die. He would give her no choice.

He was confident that his definition of the word *responsible* was beyond what Webster had intended it to be, but since Webster was long dead, it made no difference. It was his rules, his list, and his personal responsibility to stalk his chosen victims, abduct and torment them, and then murder them in cold blood.

It had been days now since he had shoved her in the trunk of his car and dragged her inside the warehouse. The police seemed to have hit a dead end in finding this missing woman, his next victim. And even though they discovered her car, they had no evidence, no clues as to her whereabouts.

This sleepy town needs a freaking wake-up call on taking care of their own. They are so self-absorbed that they can't step out of their own pathetic lives to search for a missing person. Now it's too late, as she will be yet another sad—agonizing—depressing news broadcast of a murder victim found in some remote area to report giving that sniffling piece of shit in the bad suit behind the news desk something to flap their lips about. Read the prompter—it's not that hard. Smile at the camera and win the award. They are all the same and make him sick to his stomach.

Even though he had captured his "next to kill" victim, he was stalking even the next one after that. He made his final choice and she would no doubt be easy prey. He had seen her out in the field, an investigative reporter for one of the local news stations nosing around his crime scene he had created, taking photos of his work of art behind the yellow tape, and she making her incessant notes in her tiny notepad that she kept in her top pocket of her go-to denim jacket. She had to be exceedingly shallow in so many respects to write so small, her scrunched up penmanship that nobody would be able to decipher in all probability—not even her.

She thought she knew all the facts about these murders in this small town, reporting from the field as if that was her thing, her expertise. She would stand there in front of the camera with her big hair and bleached processed white teeth and obviously had staged the backdrop for the viewer's pleasure. The camera would zoom in on the one shoe, the supposed victim's no doubt, lying there, which of course she planted to make it look good— her obvious intent to terrify the viewers of the maniac on the loose. And this was supposed to be good broadcasting? It was a set up and it, with all her efforts, would no more than bring mediocre ratings to the station and not justice to be served.

He pulled up on the handle to the aluminum siding on the door to the storage locker, looking around to see if anyone was watching him before he shut himself inside and cut himself off from the outside world. He had no choice but to borrow it from the dumb shit that left it unlocked with half of their life stuffed inside this 12 x 12 concrete hole in the wall. It had all the comforts of home.

His hideout between murders, his solitude between responsibilities.

CHAPTER TWENTY

I t had been a few days since Peter had discovered the letter from his late wife's killer buried deep inside her closet, with who knows what else she might have been hiding from him. But what he had discovered beyond the letter was not only baffling to him, but unexpected and out of character for Kate.

His disappointment and sadness were slowly turning to rage, and he now was more determined to find out what the hell was going on. For some reason something was keeping him from going to the police and his gut was signaling him to wait and do some more digging.

He knew that Big Jake didn't trust him from the moment he relinquished the ribbon key as evidence and one of the reasons that now they considered him to be a suspect. He realized a few days ago that he was being watched when he passed by an unmarked police car parked on the opposite side of his street. The officer sat there day and night watching him like a hawk, staring into his windows and surveying his every move. Maybe later today he would take him a cup of coffee just to be neighborly. After all he is in his neighborhood taking up valuable real estate so he might as well be hospitable. He could see himself tapping on the officer's window, asking him to roll it down, and hand him a hot cup of coffee out of one of his wife's favorite china cups—no words necessary, just hand it to him and walk away. A little arrogant, yes; nonetheless, would make him feel better.

He sat in deep concentration in her favorite room and even though the bloodstain had been cleaned up, it still haunted him. Perhaps he could channel her somehow. He couldn't even imagine with his closed-minded thinking that he would even come up with such a thought that he could channel his dead wife from beyond the grave. Perhaps he was going completely out of his mind crazy and wasn't even aware of *how* crazy.

He was pushing everyone away, even his own sister, Mary, who had been relentless in her phone calls and texting to the point if he didn't make an attempt to call her back and let her know he was fine, she would be knocking on his door. He couldn't deal with that right now—she would be an unwanted distraction and ask him too many questions to which he didn't have the answers to give.

His head was aching, pounding, screaming with pain on all sides as he sat thinking hard to himself about the chilling and frightening salutation of this letter to his beloved wife. The letter itself was to the point that she was next to die and his confession that he had been following her for weeks. Nonetheless, maybe she knew him, maybe she knew he was following her, but why wouldn't she tell him, her husband of all these years? He had a million questions to ask of her as to why she didn't come to him—why would she keep such a horrific secret from him and not come literally running to him with this piece of evidence, this threat on her life. Something was telling him that this was not the first letter she had received—maybe there were more and just maybe that is what Kerry Ann wanted to share with him at the coffeehouse and now she is missing and most likely dead.

He had plugged in the unfamiliar cell phone, that unexpected find that was in one of the boxes inside her closet, and impatiently watched the bars slowly charge. This finding was an unfortunate one, as he didn't realize Kate had two cell phones. *Why would she need two phones?* he kept asking himself repeatedly. He trusted his wife—he had trusted her for all these years. He held the phone in his hands and watched the bars in the corner slowly change from red to green and knew once he pressed the buttons, the truth behind this phone would come out. Was it something she was hiding from him, something she was doing behind his back? He just couldn't imagine it, not even for a moment—why he was doubting their marriage, doubting the love they had for each other.

He took a deep breath and jumped right in, pressing any and all buttons to see if he could find something—anything— that would lead him to the answers to who had killed his wife and all those other innocent women. He hoped there would be nothing to see or hear and it was just an old phone she had never traded in and just tossed aside. He was hopeful it was nothing and his trust stood to be true.

He pressed many and all buttons not finding any questionable text messages. Nonetheless, what he did discover was a saved voicemail from an unknown caller. He pressed the speaker, turned up the volume, and then hit **PLAY**. It was a man's voice, with a message to his late wife.

You looked beautiful today, Kate. I was watching you from across the street. Could you feel me close by? I wonder sometimes what you are thinking when you are running along your usual path. Are you wishing I was there with you? Are you thinking about the words I have written to you in all my letters?

I left the letter to you on your dresser this time, instead of the usual spot. Can you believe I came inside your house? I put some of your perfume on me so I could drink you in and keep you with me for the day.

I hope you are saving all my love letters, Kate, as instructed in the first one I wrote to you and hidden them where I told you to hide them. Did you? Well, I meant every word. Know this, and don't be scared, but that letter I left for you will be my last as it is time for me to move on. You will be sad, and you will miss me, but I have other responsibilities. It's important for you to understand this about me.

Peter heard the killer as he paused, then chuckled playfully, clearing his throat. His voice then switched tones from sounding like a young boy to the crazed maniac that he is. His voice deepened, the anger and frustration came through and his patience was now at zero.

You must have been worried that your freaking annoying husband hovering over your every move would find it? Well, that's just too damn bad for you, as I know you don't care about me, or anyone for that matter. Oh, and by the way, after I kill you in your own home and drag your lifeless body away—your friend will be next.

You are both dead to me.

And know this Kate—I will be back for the letters once you are gone for good and I am certain your husband will be happy to cooperate and give them back to the one that penned them.

CHAPTER TWENTY-ONE

She had hoped to be the first on the scene following the orders given by the unknown caller, but the forensics team beat her to it. The entire perimeter of the warehouse had been secured, the yellow tape strategically draped across and tied off at a tree, and the cameras were on overload shooting photos of the victim and scene from all directions. It was not surprising and total textbook.

The disappointment must have radiated off of her even behind her smoky gray sunglasses. One of the forensic team members pointed his camera in her direction, grinned one of those proud of himself grins, and clicked the shutter button, holding it down for continuous not so flattering shots.

"Parker, I see what you are doing and if I see any of those pictures on any social media site, I will personally hunt you down and kick your sorry ass."

In her subtle way, Grace flipped him off, giving him a laugh for the day, and breaking the tension of what they were facing for the next five or six hours. Parker smiled and seemed to be content with himself and not too concerned with her empty threat. He liked the attention from her any way he could get it. Although rumor had it she could kick some ass, nonetheless, this was his way of flirting with the beautiful and radiant detective. It was obvious he had a thing for her, and he wanted to ask her out, although he was too much of a chicken and publicly admitted it one late night sitting with the guys at a bar. Too much whiskey and now he had hell to pay. The guys gave him shit about it at the lab the next day, making chicken noises whenever he walked into the room. He didn't find it so amusing, however, sucked it up as best as he could. He knew the truth, and may the truth be known, the detective was hot and he didn't care what the guys did or said about it.

She took her glasses off and placed them on top of her head and then opened a stick of gum and shoved it in her mouth and then stuffed the empty wrapper back in her pocket. Her mother's voice echoed in her mind, as she had always told her and her siblings that chewing gum was not polite and no matter what and how careful you were at chewing it, you would still look like a cow chewing its cud. She had every intention of ignoring her mom's motherly advice and even though it seemed insensitive at this moment in time, chewing gum helped her focus on the task at hand and calm her nerves. The team knew to not make any snide remarks on this one, as they didn't want to piss the detective off—if that was even remotely possible.

She stared down at the gravely decomposed body inside the rusty archaic freezer and did her best to keep her composure, trying to look tough in front of the guys and not wince at the disgust and smell. She had no choice but to cover her nose with the sleeve of her jacket just for a second to move past it.

"It seems you were in the wrong place at the wrong time,

my dear, as if it would matter now," she whispered under her breath, staring down at the face of this poor innocent girl inside a metal coffin, who one day was minding her own business and now here her life over in an instant.

"Who called it in—does anyone know?" She tossed out the emphatic question to whomever was in earshot, but not directed at anyone, still staring down at this young woman, eyeing her body up and down—looking, searching for clues of who was responsible for such a horrific murder. The detective's head was spinning and stomach acid was churning as to why this psycho would want to do this to anyone.

One of the forensics blurted out the "who called it in" answer from across the warehouse. Grace had no idea who said it and didn't much care, just on the need-to-know basis.

"It was a male voice that called it in. Came in as a private caller and the person or eye witness you might say kept the phone call brief. He just said there was someone hanging around this old place that looked suspicious and to come and check it out."

"Is that right?" the detective said, sort of half-listening, but comprehending his words.

"Yes, someone called me out of the blue as well and just told me to head over here in a matter-of-fact way and then hung up. Didn't give a name, but also a male voice. Not quite sure how they got my cell number which makes no sense. Nevertheless, let's come back to that one later."

Grace signaled the forensic team on site to remove the body from the freezer, so they can get a closer look at it. She could see and Parker can shoot some photos at all angles. It took six of them to lift the freezer and adjust it just right, so they wouldn't disturb any evidence that happened to fall off her body and inside her rusty tomb. They lifted her up and out and then placed her on top of a plastic tarp. Grace didn't take her eyes off her even once, watching her body unfold as it laid to rest on the clear plastic. Forensic Detective Parker was on the ready with his camera in hand and doing his job behind the lens shooting every angle necessary. The more photos he took to put under the microscope back at the lab, the better.

"I recognize this girl," one of the detectives randomly blurted out.

"Yes, that's the girl. Her photo has been posted on the *wall of the missing* down at the station for a while now. Her stepfather has been calling at least three or four times a day wanting to know if we knew anything and had any leads to her whereabouts. His calls were expected and after a while we got used to it, poor guy."

"Well, it's unfortunate for the person that has to deliver this sad news to him, as it is not going to be easy by any stretch of the imagination. And I vote you to handle it, whoever you are, officer." Grace paused, then took one look at the officer and shooed him away, as if he was an annoying gnat, volunteering him to make this unfortunate call. He didn't look too pleased about taking an order from Detective Harper, but honestly, she didn't give a crap what he thought of her.

"Look," she said, "this isn't something a family member needs to find out from watching the six o'clock news, so suck it up and get it done fast before the news truck pulls up with camera and big lights shining all over my crime scene."

He threw his hands up on the way out of the warehouse

and mumbled some smart-ass remark about her being so pushy. She heard him—hell, everyone heard him. Again, she didn't give a crap.

Grace squatted down next to the girl's closed hand, as she had noticed something was sticking out of it.

"Parker, get down here with me and look. Be ready to shoot it with that big lens of yours." They both squatted down beside the victim and with her gloved hand she carefully opened it to see what she was holding inside. A small piece of glass lay in the palm of the dead girl's hand and Grace picked it up to take a closer look.

"Someone bring me some light. Doesn't matter, just any light," Grace barked out to the team with a desperate plea in her voice. Parker handed her his phone, the light already on.

Grace held the light in her hand and pointed down at the bloody wound. "What the hell is this?" she asked, without expecting an answer. She grabbed a towel from one of the officers standing nearby and wiped away the blood so they can get a better look at what was in her hand.

"Oh, my God. It looks like she tried to carve something in her hand; a series of numbers and letters—B12 is as far as she got. She had to have known that she was going to die. She sent a message to whomever would find her dead body. This is so incredibly sad, yet it pisses me off even more."

"What do you think it means, detective?" Parker asked.

"I am not sure, but she was frantically trying to tell us something—this was a clue to finding her killer. I give her so much credit. Smart girl … "

CHAPTER TWENTY-TWO

He circled around her like a crazed animal trapped inside a cage. They both now were behind aluminum doors, inside the borrowed—more like stolen—12 x 12, his hideout, his haven.

The threat of the storm in the distance had finally pushed its way through and the wind and rain was now pounding the crap out of the roof of the building and rattling the door, making it sound like something was twisting it like a tin can. The deafening noise was interrupting his thoughts and making him even more agitated. At this point, he was inches from stepping off a steep cliff and losing the control he had worked so hard keeping at bay.

His hands were up in the air, waving and flailing about and his mouth spewed out nasty profanities, screaming at her, his prey whom he had left behind at the warehouse. Now here she is, curled up in the center of this small space, vulnerable to the hands of a crazy man, the hands of a killer.

His every intention was to go back for her and strangle the life out of her, so he could move on to the next one on his list, his next victim in play. He had waited too long and it was obvious the schedule he was keeping had gone astray. This unwanted interruption was disconcerting and an inconvenience—one that made his blood boil. This would send him back to his refined list of responsibilities.

He squatted down next to her and lowered his voice to a whisper. She didn't flinch or even move at all. Her hands and feet were tied up, her mouth was gagged with some sort of old rag he found in one of the boxes that was shoved up against the wall. Her eyes were shut tight and to him, it appeared she was unconscious, but this didn't keep him from reprimanding her behavior, coherent or not.

"How could you? How could you think for one second that any of my victims would or could escape from me? Nobody freaking escapes from me—not ever! You my dear, have crossed the line and I don't allow anyone to cross me.

He took a seat next to her and placed his hand on her head and then ran his fingers through her long blonde hair, petting and stroking her, all while continuing his rant of fury and frustration.

"You know I went back to finish you off today. And what do I find? My warehouse monopolized by the entire police force and news media. You tainted my crime scene, you ruined this for me. I was on a schedule and now you have caused me more delays. I stayed hidden and waited for the last detective to pull away, crawled under the yellow tape and pushed my way inside the warehouse. And you? You were nowhere to be found. I searched all over for you, listening to the fish bones crush under my boots and the rats squealing at me from the rafters—searching, panting like a thirsty dog.

"Can you imagine my disappointment after all the hard work it took me to get you there? I find it maddening that the idiotic authorities didn't think to look beyond the warehouse where I found you in the reeds, passed out from what do you think—dehydration or perhaps starvation? I did leave you there for a few days without anything to drink or eat. That wasn't very considerate of me was it?" He asked the question as a matter of fact and not expecting an answer.

"Doesn't matter anymore, I suppose, because you are off my list and I am officially done with you. It's time to move you to the beach, the same place where they found your friend, Kate. Isn't it ironic that they will find you in the exact location as your best friend—you, my Responsible Number Seven? Oh, please don't worry your pretty little head too much. I am sure you will get a decent funeral service and they will say nice things about you. The good people of this town will come together in their best clothes and pay their respects to you and your sister. Wendy is it? She will be there next to you. Dead of course, but nonetheless next to you. Maybe they can have a double funeral. I am deeply sorry for your loss, but I couldn't have her barge into this town and start messing things up for me. It is such a huge responsibility that I must uphold, so I pushed her car off the side of the road. It is unfortunate for her she hit a tree and sailed through the windshield head first. I gotta tell you," he said, and then shook his head in a disbelief of his own action. "That gash on her forehead looked deep and the probability of her surviving that was zero to none. I give her a few hours and she will for sure bleed out and die from this unfortunate accident. Someone will find her car and her mangled body and then what is done is done.

"Well, listen to me ramble on. You must be bored out of your mind by now. Enough talk, as it's time go … "

He rolled her limp body up in a blanket and not giving it a second thought, dragged her out into the storm …

CHAPTER TWENTY-THREE

P eter woke up at sunrise still with the tainted letter in his grasp, his fingers holding on so tight, they were beginning to turn a not so healthy shade of blue. It was the black and white of the words that spoke the truth. Nevertheless, it was the voice of his wife's killer that will haunt him forever.

During the night he had played the voicemail repetitively from the cell phone he had found in Kate's closet. He had to assume she had hidden it from him. However, it was only speculation that his wife of all these years would have hidden anything from him and the thought of it made him feel guilty, especially now that she was gone. They had a strong relationship and trusted in each other about all things in their life and marriage. He had so many questions to ask her and so many things to tell her that happened in the past few weeks and knew there was nothing he could do to get her back.

One thing he could do is catch her killer and put him behind bars for the rest of his pathetic life. What was giving him some peace of mind was he now had in his hands the voice of the killer and the written words he can turn over to the detective as soon as possible. It was unfortunate that he memorized every nauseating word of this psycho's scratchy disgusting voice. He was certain it would be etched in his mind until his own dying day.

He had fallen asleep sometime after 2 a.m. once again at his desk, which if he had to give it a number, would be the third time this week. It seems at all times, he is surrounded by the piles of newspaper clippings he had collected over the past several weeks and his implausible amount of notes and what was in his mind, hopeful leads not only about the death of his wife, but those who had accompanied her with their own sad and tragic stories.

Not too far from his reach was a bottle of Jack Daniels. It was his good buddy Jack that was keeping him company these days and doing a crappy job of numbing his constant reality of what was now considered to be his everyday life. This obsessive need to play the role of "the detective" even took him by surprise and if he had to explain it to anyone, especially himself, it had to be his alter ego.

He stared blankly at the empty bottle of whiskey, sending his mind off the case for a few refreshing moments mesmerized by the prism of light reflecting and bouncing and dancing off his desk and around the bottle. He thought about his alter ego for a bit, finding it somewhat entertaining, and for a short period of time even considered coming up with a fictionalized character's name to give himself. He knew he would beat out Big Jake hands down and come up with something spectacular, but he figured Columbo was out of the questionand already taken. He cracked a smile for a moment and then brushed the ridiculous thought away.

On the dusty bookshelf across the room were scattered picture frames of Kate and him. One of his favorites was of Kate and Bentley he had taken at one of the 5k runs she ran while here in Chatham. She had squatted down next to Bentley holding up the first place ribbon, all smiles and so proud of herself for her accomplishment. Her beautiful smile he missed and adored so much. Such sweet happy memories now torn apart from such a tragedy, his life empty and memories now tainted by her death. He was certain he would never be able to get over her murder and even more determined to find her killer and whatever she might have been keeping from him, her husband of all these years.

Bentley lay on the sun porch outwardly annoyed at his master for waking him up so early. He hadn't been the same since Kate died and was more of a slug these days and not his normal chipper self. However, he still managed to keep his favorite ball close by just in case. He had to attribute it to the lack of exercise since he had run several miles a day alongside Kate, her running partner and confidant. For Bentley and Kate, it was love at first sight that day they met at the pound. However, if he had to make a wager on this deal of who chose whom, it was paws down for this guy. He had it bad for Kate, as she was his everything, his chosen one.

Peter managed to get up from his uncomfortable desk chair and walk his aching bones over to Bentley and give him a pat on the head.

"Maybe a walk later, buddy. What do you say? It will do us both some good."

His head was now noticeably pounding, which he immediately attributed to his good buddy, Jack, so he apologized out loud to Bentley for the delay in their walk and headed toward the kitchen to make coffee and pop a couple of aspirin. Bentley raised his eyebrows, sighed, and closed his eyes once again, not giving much thought to whatever his master was talking about.

Peter stood at the kitchen window and turned on the faucet, mindlessly filling up the coffee pot with hot water when it dawned on him that the undercover police car was no longer parked in its usual location as a permanent fixture on his street. After all, it was his job to keep a watchful eye on, and in his opinion, the unsuspecting suspect behind closed doors.

"Where are you hiding out, detective?" he mumbled to himself.

Peter stretched his neck toward the window, straining to get a glimpse of the street between a few overgrown shrubberies, but it was obvious he wasn't in plain view. Maybe he drove off to grab a cup of coffee from the convenient store or he decided on his own that Peter was innocent of any crime, especially that of killing his wife. Regardless, the officer didn't seem too concerned about Peter Foster, the suspect on Briggs Way.

He shook his head at the thought of it and counted out the coffee grounds sort of haphazardly, not so much as to be so accurate in the number of scoops to water, when he heard the screen door open and slam shut.

"What the hell" he said, jumping out of his skin, sending his heart racing. He sprinted toward the porch before realizing that Bentley didn't give him fair warning. Come to find out, he was gone.

Peter opened the screen door and stepped out and onto the cold deck floor in his bare feet frantically calling out and whistling for Bentley to come back. The two short whistles were code for Bentley and he typically obeyed, but maybe he wasn't in earshot.

"Bentley always had a thing for those yellow tennis balls and didn't care who threw it as long as someone did. Isn't that right, Mr. Foster?"

Peter stood there frozen in his stance, on the ready to turn around when his move was interrupted by the voice of this intruder—the familiar, disgusting, and scratchy voice of a killer. Then he realized that it was him, his wife's abductor and murderer—he was standing just inches from him. He started to turn his body around to get a look at this guy, but the killer stopped him immediately.

"I wouldn't bother to turn around, because I will kill you and whoever gets in my way."

"Oh, and not to worry about giving me the two-cent tour, because I know this old house well. Been here a few times maybe three or four, but who's counting."

"I need you on your knees now, Mr. Foster—do it!"

The intruder stepped outside on the deck and pointed a gun at the back of Peter's head, his hands outwardly shaking and asked the one question that had been on his mind.

"Where are the letters?"

"What letters? I don't know what you are talking about. What did you do with my dog?"

"Keep your head down and step back inside. We are going to search this house together and once we find the letters that

I wrote to your beloved Kate, we will be taking what I call a little joy ride."

"Oh, and that police officer outside that was what I must assume was protecting you, he won't be coming to your rescue, as I made sure of that with my bare hands when he took his last breath."

CHAPTER TWENTY-FOUR

He left me there for dead. That psycho who has been killing all these women, including my best friend, he thought I was unconscious and unaware of my surroundings. He assumed I wasn't listening to his every word while I laid there curled up inside that horrific, dark, evil room while he hovered over me as if I was his prize. He thought I wasn't paying attention to every detail of his face, his voice, his slimy demeanor. He thought he was smarter than me. He chose the wrong person, the wrong girl, and he will pay for all the mistakes along his gruesome path.

She knew in her mind she wasn't just thinking these thoughts—she was having a conversation with someone in the room. Nonetheless, she was in a deep sleep as if she was floating above herself. She could hear muffled voices around her and the unremitting beeping of machines and monitors that surrounded her hospital bed. There was a pressure around her arm, which gave her comfort somehow. She finally felt safe, or more like saved.

"How long has she been out?" Detective Harper asked the nurse at the victim's bedside. The nurse's head was down, busying herself by adjusting the patient's blood pressure cuff and updating her chart with medical jargon.

The nurse purposely didn't look up from what she was doing, as her allegiance was to her patient's needs, not to the detective's. She wanted to concentrate on her patient needs and not the detective glaring at her from across the room.

"I would have to say five or six hours now." The nurse took a guess on that one to appease the detective for the moment, as she could feel her attitude seeping off the cold shoulder she was giving her. She hoped her comment would deflect the next question.

"You know they found this poor woman on the beach just like the others, but this time instead of taking her directly to the morgue, they brought her to my floor where she is being given the best care." The nurse kept her head down, not giving the detective eye contact.

"Yes, I realize she was found on the beach, as I am the one who found her."

The nurse turned around and faced the detective, crossing her arms over her chest, and came to the conclusion she needed to pay attention, so she waited for her to continue.

"Oh, I didn't know you were the one that found her and alive, which is a miracle in itself."

Detective Harper moved in closer to the victim, placed both hands on the bed railing, and continued telling her story to the now attentive nurse.

"It seems as though our killer is getting sloppy and it was my assumption by this so called sloppiness that he or she, mind you, is conveying they have started to panic. The mistakes are piling up, which means the tiredness is setting in fast. The more mistakes killers make, the more they want to get caught. You see, he (or she, I want to add) thought they killed this one, but failed to do so."

The detective stared down into the victim's face, now a patient of this hospital and a witness to such unspeakable crimes and whispered, "You got lucky, my dear!"

"Do you recognize her, Detective Harper?"

"Oh, yes! Without a doubt. I know of this woman, but not on a personal level. Just that she had been abducted, missing, and now found. So grateful!"

"You are so right—she is so lucky, detective."

"Do you mind if I have a few minutes with her, you know, to see if I can get her to tell me anything about the identity of the maniac that did this to her?"

"Of course not, but a warning to you, because I know how you push. Rumor has it from the other nurses on this staff that you are relentless to our patients when it comes to pumping them for the slightest of information. I am begging you to take it easy on this one, as she has been through a lot."

"Listen, you don't need to concern yourself with my tactics and I don't need to qualify my so-called 'pushing' to you or anyone else on this staff. What I need from you is to make sure this doesn't leak out to the press that she is alive.

"I wasn't exactly asking for your permission from you or this hospital. It is imperative that this killer thinks she is dead. I want the killer to think they can move on to the next victim. I don't want this maniac wandering the halls of this hospital searching for her and finishing her off for good. Don't let anyone at the news desk know about this. If they must lie about her well-being, do it! I need you to take care of this."

The nurse glared at the detective with disbelief, trying to comprehend why she wanted her to lie and why the news media wasn't alerted or on the scene of this crime in the first place. The police kept this one locked up in a tight drum.

The detective continued her orders.

"Call that journalist at the TV station—you know the one that has been on this case and out in the field mucking up my crime scenes. What's her name? Olivia Fox? Have her report from the beach, the same beach that the other victims were found and then the killer will feel vindicated and move on to his next kill. Make sure you sound convincing, so this Ms. Fox doesn't catch on. She is on my crime scenes like white on rice and she is pissing me off more and more every day. Got it?"

That comment seemed to shut up the nurse in a hurry and with the hardcore list of detailed instructions given by the obnoxious and beyond demanding detective, she turned on her practical shoes and exited the room. Clearly by the rush of red to her face, she was pissed off and ready to scratch someone's eyes out, anyone that happened to get in her way.

Detective Harper moved on with her itinerary and list of questions and pulled up a chair to the hospital bed, sitting as close as possible, taking the victim's hand in hers. She studied this poor woman's swollen face and the many black and blue marks all over her body that undoubtedly exemplified a map of the terrifying chain of events that happened to her in the past few days. She squeezed her eyes closed and could see flashes of what might have happened to this poor soul lying in this bed.

She leaned in and whispered her name.

"Kerry Ann, can you hear me?" Not waiting for her response, she continued.

"My name is Detective Harper and I am here to help you and this town catch the son-of-a-bitch that did this to you. What can you tell me, if anything, about where we can find this maniac that is killing the women of this town and that abducted you and tortured you?"

Kerry was listening to her every word and the questions she asked. She turned her head toward the detective's voice, her eyes swollen shut, and moaning, as the pain was excruciating.

She pulled her parched lips apart and managed to let out a slight whisper, "You must catch him. He is dangerous and he will find me—I know it." Her eyes were still closed, but her tears managed to seep out and slide down her cheeks.

"We are working on that, I promise, Kerry Ann. He has killed at least five people now, all women. You are the lucky one, Lucky Number Six."

Kerry opened her eyes and stared into the detective's blurry face and continued telling her story. "You can't let him know that I am here. He will find me—I can feel it."

Although her voice now sounds panicked and desperate, she manages to get out one of the most important facts of this case so far. "He is behind the silver door, you will find him behind the silver door, that is where he took me and he hides out like a coward."

Kerry Ann drifted off again, leaving the detective sitting there feeling frustrated and still without answers.

"Look, I need you to try and stay awake," the detective

demanded, still holding onto her hand. She squeezed it ever so slightly and Kerry took a deep breath, grimaced, and then opened her swollen eyes again.

"Good. Good, that's it! Thank you. Thank you for trying. I realize that you are exhausted and terrified, but the bottom line is that I need more. Think real hard. Go back to the place in your mind and try to see something. Try to remember your surroundings. What were the sounds beyond this silver door? Did you hear water or maybe smelled smoke or chemicals from the smoke stacks from the industrial buildings that are on the north side? You know that area of town, I am sure, since it's close to the dunes where the police officers found your car."

The passion in the detective's voice was beyond the call of duty. Kerry could sense something else was driving this woman to find out more for another reason. Revenge perhaps. Pure determination. Her voice resonated in Kerry's brain as she desperately tried to recall the horrific happenings that her captor did to her in that dark dank tin can hole in the wall and even in the abandoned warehouse where he first left her for several days—the same place she found the dead body inside the freezer.

Kerry Ann was so tired and her bruised ribs made it difficult to breathe, let alone talk. Her voice was raspy, nonetheless, she managed to utter a few more words that would be vital to this case.

"Okay, I'll try. There were silver double doors or maybe it was one, it is hard to say. Above the door was a rusty plate with numbers engraved on the plaque. They were difficult to decipher, but B121—something like that.

Kerry paused and swallowed hard and then continued.

"When he opened the door, it sounded like one of those garage doors. Inside was a bunch of boxes and furniture stacked as high as the ceiling itself. He tossed me inside like I was a piece of trash. I thought I remembered what he looked like, but all I see is shadows in my head. Maybe if I wasn't so tired, I could remember more—I am truly sorry."

"You did good, Kerry Ann, you did real good."

The detective squeezed her hand one more time, giving her reassurance.

"Don't worry, because I will come back to see you when you are stronger. I plan to bring my sketchpad and then perhaps you will remember what this killer looks like, down to every slimy detail. You are obviously in shock and that shock is preventing you from seeing his true identity, this monster that abducted and tormented you and killed all those innocent women."

"Get some rest now."

She turned with the intentions of letting go of Kerry's hand and walking away, however, she felt a squeeze that stopped her in her stance.

"Detective, you have to try and contact my sister. He told me she was dead and in some horrific car accident. Please tell me that isn't true. Please tell me it was just another lie oozing from his evil mind."

"Her name is Wendy, Wendy Hill—please find her for me. She can't be dead. She's all I have left."

CHAPTER TWENTY-FIVE

Detective Grace Harper made it a point upon her exit of the hospital to take the stairs rather than the sluggish ride on the elevator. Her car, if she remembered correctly, was parked on the fourth level on the northeast corner of the parking garage. She typically made it a habit to take a photo of the sign indicating which floor number she parked on so she wouldn't forget. Nothing like feeling like an idiot when trying to search for your car on every level. Unfortunately for her, today she forgot to take the photo. This happens when the mind is scattered, so she could only hope she would be spot on with her recall.

Grace felt somewhat relieved from what she was able to pull out of Kerry Ann about her captor, yet in shock at this new twist to this already twisted case. A sister now in play either dead or missing at the hands of this maniac or maybe she doesn't exist at all. Kerry could be delusional at this point from all the pain medication and trauma she experienced, however, now after meeting her, she felt even more compelled to check out her story.

There was so much to report to her partner, and she was

feeling overly anxious to get to the station. By the looks of the ten missed calls on her cell phone, it appeared that Big Jake had been trying to get in touch with her for quite some time now. Her intent was to head in that direction and report what she had learned from the patient in hospital room 417. She had way too much to divulge to put up with Big Jake's wrath and was hoping she could just push through his load of crap and give it to him straight.

Kerry Ann was one of the lucky ones to survive the maniac that was terrorizing the women of this town and even though she was bruised and swollen, she would recover from her bodily injuries without any complications, however, her memory of this horrific nightmare will forever be stained in her mind. She could so relate to this permanent stain with her own family tragedy—maybe this is why she had such a connection with the victim.

Kerry was now in good hands at the hospital thanks to Grace appointing a 24-hour security guard at her door, which would give her and the hospital staff a sense of relief knowing she had police protection. She was most certain she would catch hell, as it would no doubt cost the department more than pocket change.

Once the killer discovers that he didn't succeed in killing Kerry Ann, his Responsible Number Six, there is no telling what he would do next. How could he have left her at that beach and not finished her off? He was getting more than sloppy and will want to clean up this mess somehow. He will either find Kerry Ann or choose another.

Grace descended the steel-framed staircase and with more

strength in her body that she could imagine, she shoved the door open and entered the fourth level. The combination of her adrenalin rush and the heavy door sent the door sailing and then slamming up against the concrete wall. The echo giving her a shiver down her spine. This murder investigation has made her more than on edge and it was time to solve it.

Her car is now sitting solo exactly where she thought she parked it, but she felt somewhat creeped out. As she briskly walked toward her car, her keys in hand, she felt like she was being watched. Most likely her imagination, as if she had a part in a bad plot to a scary movie. It was time to get the hell out of here and onto the streets of Chatham.

Grace pulled out into the traffic, but merging into the left lane flipping on her turn signal, she missed the light by a couple seconds.

"Damn this light, it never fails that I hit this thing every time," she muttered to herself, hitting the steering wheel with her fist. She was only a couple of miles from the police station at this point and her anxiety had elevated to the next level. Her heart was doing that flip flop thing it did back when her sister was killed. It was all too familiar, so she tried her best to push it down like she always did when it came to her emotions.

She took the time allotted at the pain in the ass long light, put on her sunglasses, and then adjusted the rearview mirror. Something caught her attention in the mirror—or rather someone.

The light turned green and she did her best to keep an eye on the road and the vehicle behind her. It was following close, yet abiding by the one car length between. From what she could make out, the silhouette of the driver looked like a male. Then her assumption was confirmed when he rolled down the window, sticking out his hairy arm, followed by a trail of smoke from either a cigar or cigarette.

As the driver pulled up alongside her, staying with her exact speed, she glanced over to see if she could get a better look at the asshole behind the wheel. Realizing at this point it was a taxi cab, she felt somewhat relieved, nonetheless, still on alert as to why her final destination was so pertinent to his agenda. He turned his attention directly at her, his eyes shielded by a dark pair of sunglasses and a baseball cap pulled down low over his face. He took a big drag on his fat stogie and blew smoke deliberately at her, the smoke filling the entire front seat of his cab and camouflaging his identity even more so.

She was stunned by this creep's unnecessary gesture and found herself slamming on her brakes, just barely missing the car in front of her.

"What an asshole," she yelled out loud, flipping him off at the same time.

She pulled into the police station parking lot, happy the cab kept on moving down the road. It was time to come clean with her partner and let him know that Kerry Ann was alive.

CHAPTER TWENTY-SIX

Big Jake sat at his cluttered desk shuffling papers around and studying the contents of the files of the women that are now dead at the hands of this wanted criminal.

The killer's calling card was now confirmed at the warehouse crime scene, as he had left his signature in a simple note, as if he was jotting down items on a grocery list. The note was pinned neatly onto the victim's clothing for the criminal investigators to discover what he had casted himself to be in this diminutive play of murders he was directing. It was obvious he wanted to get caught and was enjoying leaving the necessary breadcrumbs that lead the investigators to the scene. He thrived on the chase, he thrived on the stage presence.

"The Responsible One," he dubbed himself, was purposely ending the lives of these innocent women he had randomly selected off the streets of Chatham, as if it was his own personal lottery. Adding a number to each note was a key factor in solving this equation as to how many victims he had killed so far. Easy math to solve, but not so easy to find the one who was responsible, aka "the Responsible One." The name he had given himself was certainly a far cry from the Oceanside Strangler, some cheap toss out the anchor took credit for on the local news. Nothing to be proud of, however, the effort was noted.

Big Jake had solved many cases in his twenty some years on the force and witnessed some horrific murder scenes, nevertheless, this one had blown him away beyond comprehension. Each murder was so similar, yet the more this person murdered, the more the tactics changed, which made it even more difficult for investigators to fit the pieces together. At this time this lunatic had no rhyme or reason as to the whys these women were being killed, however, the killer is still compelled to do it and get the job done.

Big Jake called an impromptu meeting an hour prior asking the obligatory questions of the other detectives on this case, only to get disappointing answers. Most disappointing was not seeing his partner in attendance and now, after calling her more than enough times beyond frustration, his blood pressure had elevated noticeably, not so good for the obvious overly indulged.

"What exactly was she up to?" he grumbled to himself, as he was ready to dial her number again. They were supposed to be partners, and partners work together. The last time she checked in with him was when she was leaving the scene at the warehouse. And other than the calling card information the killer left behind, she owed him a list of details from the hours she spent behind the crime scene tape.

He rubbed both sides of his temples with his stout fingers, expecting to wipe away what seemed to be the incessant ache in his head that has been permanent since the first murder victim, which took place a month ago. Time flies when you are trying to solve a murder or two. Deciding to make yet another frustrating attempt, he dialed his partner's number, but her phone immediately directed him to voicemail after the second ring. He slammed down the phone so hard he realized he could have cracked the screen. Regretful, he flipped it over, but fortunate for him, not this time.

"Damn it, Grace," he mumbled under his breath and knew her reasons as to why she felt compelled to go off on her own. However, he had to call her out on it this time, as she had no excuses anymore. She was predictable, because of her past, but a pain in his ass in the present.

A tap at the door gave Big Jake a slight startle, but mostly pissed him off as he didn't want to be disturbed. He wished now he would have closed his door all the way, locked it, and slapped a *Do Not Disturb* sign on the chipped paint.

Needless to say, it was too late for the sign and the sergeant with the so-called urgent message tapped and pushed the door open more than the necessary crack.

Big Jake's silence to his presence sent a clear and concise message, as he continued with shuffling papers. Arrogant, yes, however, necessary for this desk fly that is standing in his doorway at this moment and interrupting his train of thoughts on this case.

"Excuse me, Detective Elliott, but you have a call on Line 3."

"Is that right?"

"Yes. He says he is a cab driver. Works for Cape Cod Cruiser Company. He has called more than a dozen times and he insists that he has some information about this case."

The sergeant more than shuddered and stammered his words, but managed to get them all out eventually. It was obvious the detective made him more than a little nervous.

"Look, I honestly can't deal with another false lead right now, as I am busy having the nervous breakdown that I so deserve. Take a message, hang up on the guy, give it to one of the blues—I don't care what you do, just get out of my office."

Grace could hear the conversation all the way down the hallway. Hell, there is a good chance everyone could hear Big Jakes' boisterous pipes from the parking lot.

She pushed her way past the sergeant, who seemed to be literally taking up the entire doorway of her partner's office. She took one look at Jake and then closed the door slowly saying a quiet goodbye to the sergeant and leaving him alone in the hallway and somewhat humiliated.

Jake looked more than pissed and a little constipated—she humored herself with the thought, however, didn't say it out loud.

"Well, if it isn't the amazing Grace, fighting crime on the streets alone I see? Did you forget that we are partners and we are working on this case together? What the hell, Grace, you purposely ignored my, what, I lost count, a dozen calls I made to you today?"

"It was actually ten. Yes, ten to be exact." She was hopeful her smart-ass response would change the rage expression on his face, so they could move past this and shift the conversation to what is more important in this moment. However, her efforts failed miserably.

"I don't find this amusing, detective."

He stood up from his desk to pace the floor and release some of his built-up rage. He accidently knocked over his cold coffee, which spilled all over his chair with a painful slow drip to the floor, his face now blood red.

"Jake, look, I know you are angry, and I am so sorry. However, I have to say there are several unfortunate, but good reasons why I have been off the grid. I should say, why Parker and I both have been off the grid. I am prepared to give you the play-by-play right now."

"Parker, really? Why Parker? He is an asshole, Grace—you shouldn't have dragged him along with you, as he can be a snitch and say things he shouldn't to all the wrong people."

"Yes, you are so right on that, Jake, however, in this instance, he was a huge help to me today. As much as he annoys me, I am grateful he was there. I trust him, Jake, and you know me, so you need to trust me on making this call to drag him along."

"Well, like my coffee, spill your guts and do it fast, as my patience is running thin."

CHAPTER TWENTY-SEVEN

Grace took a seat in one of the tattered-looking garage sale chairs and scooted it in closer to Jake's desk, folding her now trembling hands in her lap. He said nothing as he sopped up the coffee spill with a wad of cheap fast food napkins he had tucked inside his middle drawer and then tossing the soaked heap carelessly into his already over-stuffed garbage can.

Her mind was spinning as to where to start this dreaded conversation. She could now feel the muscles in her neck tense up, alerting her body of the stressful, gruesome turn of events that transpired from the scene at the abandoned warehouse, to the beach, and then to the hospital.

She had to look as bad as she felt—a disheveled Grace and not the always polished look she strived to achieve on a day-to-day. Nonetheless, she earned it in more ways than one and at this point didn't care. She wondered if Jake would say something derogatory about her appearance, so she prepared herself to retaliate if necessary. He would not have any recourse on this topic and it could literally bite him in his very wide ass.

She waited for Jake to finish up with his mindless cleaning activity and to finally take a seat, giving her his full attention. He did just that and now she had no possible course of action but to spill it all, his reference to her story had to be told.

"Jake, this might not be in the exact order of how all of this came to be, however, I will do my best to lay it all out for you. It has been an exhausting day."

"Cut the crap, Grace. You are stalling on purpose and you know it."

"Okay, okay, you are right. It was almost sunset by the time we wrapped things up at the warehouse. The body of the young woman found inside the freezer had already been bagged and tagged by the forensics team and they, along with the other blues, had vacated the premises."

"There was just one other person hanging around besides me, shooting as many photos as possible, or more like biding time to get me alone."

"Parker?" Jake interjected with a snarky tone.

"Yes, Parker. I am sure you have heard the rumors at the hypothetical 'water cooler' about his obsession he has with me, right?"

"Don't flatter yourself Grace. He is still an asshole in my book. Please get over it. What is he, twelve at most?"

"C'mon, Jake, I get it. You have mentioned on more than one occasion that Parker is an asshole and I have been informed and now am fully aware. So freaking stop patronizing me and give me a break. I have a lot to say and you will know all that happened. Just hear me out."

"Look, I wasn't happy about him hanging around the

warehouse and I hadn't planned on giving him the time of day—hell, I just wanted him to do his job like all of us.

"But then something came over me and my strong intuition that you are so familiar with hit me so hard. I felt that rush of overwhelming panic that took me back to that horrific day when I found my sister lying dead on the cold concrete floor of my childhood home. I had this feeling about Kerry Ann that she was able to escape her captor and she was alive somewhere on the beach. I went on total heart-wrenching punch you in the stomach gut feeling."

"What are you getting at, Grace? You have got to stop this intuition bullshit. Just because you were the one that found your sister after she had been murdered doesn't mean you have some sixth sense about you. This is real life criminal investigation and you know for a fact we go on evidence and not gut or that palm reading shit you want to base this case, hell, all of our cases on."

"Really, Jake? Do me a favor, partner, don't define me because of my past. Have respect for me as a person and for what I have been through. My sister's murder, her death made me the great detective I am today. It gave me the skills I needed to find the scum on the streets and put them away for good. I plan to find this killer. And what difference does it make if it's a gut feeling or found evidence, as long as we get them off the streets and put away for good? So, again, I will ask you to stop patronizing me."

Her unyielding words seemed to shut Jake up for the moment. He was now adjusting himself in his chair and nervously swiveling back and forth, awaiting this gut feeling story with bated breath.

"I asked Parker to follow me over to the beach where most of the victims had been found all dead; of course, in that position the killer placed them in, face down in the sand, bound, with the sign pinned to their clothing."

"Parker seemed more than eager to go with me to the beach and rambled nervously about having plenty of juice left on his camera battery and flash. I didn't pay much attention to his nonsense, as my focus shifted to getting inside my vehicle and heading in that direction. Parker followed me over in his Jeep, sort of clueless of what my intentions were. I could certainly tell he was excited to use his camera and that long lens of his for the greater good."

"We still had some daylight in our favor, as it was more than possible according to, yes, my gut, we could stumble upon some evidence on the path to the beach where I was hopeful to find Kerry Ann alive.

"When we arrived, there wasn't a soul in sight, so we chose a path that looked fairly easy to navigate to our final destination without the risk of tripping over an abundance of tree roots and brush."

"It took less than five minutes to discover the body. It took eight minutes to find her. Kerry Ann, face down in the sand, bound, sign pinned to her clothes that read Responsible Number Six."

"Breathing, not dead."

"It looks as if my gut feeling paid off."

CHAPTER TWENTY-EIGHT

J ake's cell phone went off in a vibrating frenzy, sending it gyrating in circles and bringing Grace and his conversation to an abrupt interruption. The call was coming from an officer working out on the streets, so he felt compelled to answer right away. The caller was brief, message given, message received.

It didn't take long for the entire department to receive the same tragic news as they could hear their voices penetrate through the thin walls of Jake's office and see their shadows briskly passing by his window.

The chaos in the hallway only heightened Grace's frustration that she had not been included in the loop of this unexpected news.

Jake slammed the phone down on the desk, which sent him in motion of this mindless straightening the papers in front of him, with no organizational purpose. He pushed himself up slowly, as if he had a desperate ache in his joints and throughout his body. The color immediately drained from his face, when he grabbed his cell and tucked it inside his pants pocket. There was obviously somewhere else he needed to be, and it was now apparent that their meeting was over.

Grace moved up to the edge of her chair and was waiting for him to say something, anything. He was eerily quiet, and Jake is never this quiet—she had almost felt sorry for him.

"What the hell is going on, Jake? It looks as if you just heard that the world was coming to an end."

"We need to go, Grace, and right now!"

"Jake, fill me in—you are scaring me."

He looked directly at her, his eyes sort of hazy and bloodshot, and then delivered the news to her direct and hard.

"There has been another murder, Grace. A murder that is out of context of his pattern like the girl we found in the water, however, this time it's one of our officers."

"We need to head over to Peter Foster's place on Briggs Way. The officer that was assigned to protect Peter Foster is now dead. He was strangled to death inside his squad car while protecting and keeping a watchful eye on Mr. Foster. And now, Mr. Foster is nowhere to be found. This sickens me to no end that we haven't stopped this killer yet, and now it's beyond personal."

As soon as they exited Jake's office, the entire precinct was in an uproar, voices raised, shocked expressions and downright rage at this news. It was obvious that the entire department caught wind of this news that one of their brothers had fallen.

It was a short ride. Maybe fifteen minutes at best. However, for Grace it felt more like an eternity. Briggs Way was just through town and on the beach side, where most of the tourists ventured for summer vacation. It was the end of season for Chatham, so the streets were less crowded.

The silence between them was deafening and she wanted to continue their conversation of what happened next on the beach. She wanted to explain to Jake how they managed to get Kerry Ann into Parker's car and then to the hospital without anyone spotting them. However, it didn't appear to be important at this time and her story would have to wait. She found herself bringing up an entirely separate topic that had been weighing on her mind for a long time, taking advantage of Jake's quiet mood.

"You know, Jake, everyone has many layers—believe me, I figured this out the hard way. There is no perfect family by any stretch of any imagination. No perfect anything. I have never shared this with you before, but I would like you to know something while we make this unfortunate drive to Mr. Foster's residence. And don't worry, I am not expecting you to respond—just to listen."

Jake looked over at his partner in the seat next to him, giving her the head nod gesture without actually saying the words that she had the floor to tell this story that was eating her up.

"Not only did I lose my sister, but her death also ended my parents' marriage. Not exactly something my siblings and I expected to happen—my sister was an unbelievable shock, but my parents split—not a chance in the world that this would have happened. Family is supposed to come together when tragedy strikes and help each other through it, somehow working together for the greater good. However, for my parents, they just couldn't handle the stress, not even for a minute, or so it seemed. Nobody was ever the same after my sister died, especially my mother. My father left all of us and we never heard from him again. Who does that, for Christ sake?"

Grace looked out the passenger side window, so Jake wouldn't see her cry. She lightly brushed away her tears from her cheeks, took a cleansing breath, and continued.

"We all watched my mother sink into such a deep depression that no matter what we did to help her feel better, she wasn't able to come out of it. We buried her last year next to my sister. And can you believe it—my dad didn't show up to her funeral? What a coward he was for doing that to her and for doing that to his own children."

"They both have angels engraved on their gravestones, I made sure of that. They were angels on this earth and now in Heaven. Heaven is pretty damn lucky to have them."

"Is that why you have the two angels tattooed on your ankle, Grace?"

"Yes. I did that in their honor. Never thought you noticed."

Jake reached over and squeezed her hand, the first physical sign of compassion that he had shown since they became partners. Grace took in another deep breath and felt somewhat relieved that her partner would show some compassion. She knew he had it in him somewhere.

The main road to Peter Foster's house had been closed to everyone except police, paramedics, and forensics, the obvious people permitted beyond the barricades. Jake had to do some fancy maneuvering to get to the side street where everyone seemed to be gathered. This was the wing of the house that had the spectacular view of the lush backyard, wraparound porch, and the big tree with the swing. Beyond the tree and straight down the steep hill was a spectacular private beach complete with a row of canopies and white Adirondack chairs. This property was breathtaking by any stretch of the imagination and it was obvious that the Fosters paid the big bucks for the land and the house on top of it.

Grace still had trust issues with this Peter Foster character and questioned if he had something to do with his wife's death. She was the first one to die in this string of murders and there have not been any other tangible leads to her killer or to the others. For some reason she suspected Mr. Foster, especially after seeing him nosing around down by the pier and making himself at home during their investigation of the young woman that washed up next to the dock. How he dared go beyond the crime scene tape tossing on the baseball cap seemed suspicious, wanting to blend in like he owned the joint, like he was one of them. On the other hand, his beloved wife had been brutally murdered, and people do crazy shit when something so tragic happens to a loved one. She hoped this time her gut was completely off, and he was just trying to get justice for his wife's murder.

They walked up together and joined the circle of investigators already in a briefing of what had been discovered inside the house and out.

Jake leaned into Grace and whispered that her boyfriend was here. She didn't find it funny and shushed him immediately. She would have to admit it was a good ice breaker to move past the disagreement between the two of them. She felt Parker's eyes on her and glanced over at him, his camera in hand and a smile on his face.

Jake interrupted the officer already in full discussion of what had been discovered on the property, beyond the officer who was found dead inside his vehicle in front of the house.

"Officer Jenkins, can you fill us in please?" Jake asked.

"Sure, detectives," Officer Jenkins said, welcoming the two of them to the circle.

"Like I was saying, someone had called in a noise ordinance of a barking dog. When we pulled up, we could hear not just a barking dog, but one who was in major distress. The dog was tied to the tree behind me, but once untied, ran inside the ransacked house. At the same time, this is when we found Officer Bradly inside his squad car strangled to death.

"Mr. Foster was nowhere in sight and the house has been literally turned upside down. He is not just gone—he has been taken."

"What makes you think that, detective?"

"There was a note inside the house that read:"

> *Looking for Mr. Foster?*
> *He is presently in the trunk of my car.*
>
> *Yours truly,*
> *The Responsible One …*

CHAPTER TWENTY-NINE

He pulled into the gated facilities by punching in the necessary code and then slithered his vehicle in between the narrow alleyways until he approached the 12 x 12, he has called home for the past few weeks.

At this point, the cab he had so-called "borrowed" from the lot had overheated and unfortunate for him was leaving a trail of smoke from the engine this time, and not his nasty cigar.

It didn't appear that anyone was on the premises tending to crap they left behind inside one of these tin cans, nonetheless, he was taking a risk of getting caught in broad daylight.

Thinking back to what just took place at Peter Foster's, he had to admit he found it entertaining leaving the notes on his victims' dead bodies for the authorities to discover. Now the smart-ass note he left inside Mr. Foster's house he considered to be a bonus. He had to give them some sort of breadcrumbs to follow, since they were doing such a crappy job of finding any clues. He had to attend to his list of responsibilities, knowing that he had the cops on this trail made his line of work more interesting. Just to think, he had this secret life for so long. Business owner in this small town for all these years and a killer—seemed to him to be an impressive resume. He was astonished that the towns' people hadn't figured out that he was a killer.

He stepped outside of the cab and his steel-toed boots came down hard on the gravel ground. He took one more look at his surroundings and then walked over to the trunk, putting his head down close to listen intently to see if there were any more banging noises coming from his abducted prey.

It seemed that the noises had come to an end, as the quiet was deafening. The thought had crossed his psychotic mind that when he opened the trunk maybe his captive would be stone-cold dead, so he wouldn't have to waste his time on this piece of shit.

To his disappointment, Peter was alive and glaring up at his abductor, gasping for the much-needed air that filtered inside once the trunk was open.

"Let's get one thing straight, you sick bastard, I will kill you with my bare hands if it is the last thing I do on this earth. You are beyond delusional and I hope they put you away for a long time," Peter said, still having difficulty breathing.

"You don't have the strength to take me down, old man. You are wasting my time, as I have better things to do."

He then turned toward the aluminum doors and keyed the small padlock, pulling the handle up to open the garage door part way before reaching back to grab his unexpected prisoner. He was looking forward to telling Peter all about his dead wife and what they shared together behind these doors.

Peter sat in the corner with his hands and feet tied, anticipating what was about to come next. He watched this guy pace the concrete floor, moving things around in a chaotic manor and rifling through some of the boxes he had to assume didn't belong to him. This psychopath was beyond crazy and Peter knew what he was capable of doing to his wife and others.

Now that he was inside this cold damp space, he couldn't help but envision what his beloved Kate must have gone through and how terrified she had to have been in the presence of this killer, her murderer. He wanted things to be different—he wanted his Kate back—he wanted the impossible.

"What do you want from me? You have already taken my wife away from me—just kill me and get it over with, so I don't have to suffer this loss anymore. Or are you a coward?"

The killer sat down on a small crate across from Peter and pulled out a cigar from his top shirt pocket and stared at it for a while, seemingly in deep thought, ignoring his prisoner's ridiculous questions and concerns. He slowly ran the cigar under his nose, closing his eyes and inhaling the aroma of his most precious addiction. He was surprisingly calm, and arrogance was oozing off of him like the stench of the cancer stick in his hand.

"Do you know what goes well with this type of cigar, Mr. Foster? Bourbon. That's right, either on the rocks or not, doesn't much matter to me. Honestly, I am not much of a drinker, but certainly keep a few cases of these bad boys at arm's length. You like to pour yourself a strong one, don't you, Mr. Foster? Yes. Kate told me that you are a Jack Daniels drinker, especially when you are feeling melancholy. You open up a bottle of Jack and drink all night mumbling obscenities under your breath, pissed off for all the world's uncertainties you cannot fix. Especially your marriage—isn't that right, Mr. Foster? Isn't that right, Peter?"

He didn't expect him to give him an answer, but just sat there twisting the Victor Sinclair 55 series cigar wrapper between his slimy filthy fingers and read the numbers imprinted on the wrapper over and over under his breath.

"It seems I can be careless sometimes and I am not sure you know that about me, Mr. Foster, but I tend to leave these little suckers laying around. I left one in Kerry Ann's car on the floor of the backseat after abducting her from the alleyway behind her business, and yet, they still haven't solved this case. It is quite the head scratcher, as they have had plenty of opportunities to figure this out. I watch the news daily and that weasel behind the news desk is on repeat about not having any leads on this case. Hell, what is the matter with them that they can't find me? I find it entertaining to say the least."

"Listen to me, shooting the shit like we are friends. What the hell am I thinking? I need to pull it together and get back on topic. My topic of choice would be Kerry Ann. You know her, right, Mr. Foster?"

"No need to respond as I already know the answer. Your wife told me you hadn't really been introduced properly, but you would wave from just enough distance between you so you wouldn't have to make nice with her best friend. What— were you jealous she wasn't giving you the time of day? You hated the fact that your wife took care of herself and she was attractive. You absolutely despised her running every day and that you weren't able to keep an eye on her and know where she was at all times. You wanted to control her didn't you?"

He paused for a few minutes twisting the cigar wrapper around on his finger.

"God, she looked good and felt good in my arms."

"You are delusional, and I don't know what the hell you are talking about. My wife would never be touched by you, you sick bastard. You are making no sense to me and I know my wife and she wouldn't have anything to do with you. She was a victim and you killed her in cold blood. Someone needs to admit you to a padded cell and feed you through a small hole. You should never see the light of day again."

Peter tried to stand, but before he could get to his feet, as awkward as it was while tied up, his captor shoved him back down with the heel of his boot. When he landed hard on his side, his captor kicked him as hard as he could in the stomach. Peter yelled out in pain.

"I am afraid you are not going anywhere. Try that shit again and I will hit you so much harder and that's a promise. And why would I make any sense to you or anyone? I am a psychopath—remember? You said it yourself. Once I tend to my daily work and my responsibilities, I will figure out what to do with you at that time. You will be staying here in this place, so my home is now your home until I am done with you."

He threw his head back in laughter, one of those sinister laughs that was so surreal it couldn't have come from any sane person.

He then admitted to his prisoner that he left that cigar wrapper on the floor of Kerry Ann's car on purpose so the authorities would get a freaking clue.

"Mr. Foster, you know for a fact that the authorities don't

know what they are doing. You know this as truth, because you have been out there mucking up my crime scenes with your half-assed detective skills. You do know that you are not a detective, right? Hell, the detectives that supposedly know what they are doing have no leads, no clues, and they don't have any sense in their brains as to find a serial killer. What they don't realize is that I will keep killing these women and then the police officer, because he was in my way, and now you—just for pure entertainment."

CHAPTER THIRTY

H er eyes snapped open in a panic as she began to search the unfamiliar room. It was pitch dark and she had to make more than an effort to focus on anything in this space that made sense to her. It was completely different from the rat-infested warehouse her abductor had left her in for what seemed like days on end, as well as the place that he referred to as the 12 x 12.

In this moment she felt lucid in a sense of mind, however, her body felt heavy somehow, trapped—even paralyzed. Maybe he drugged her or even poisoned her, and this was how it felt to die a slow painful death.

There was a high-pitched beeping noise above her and since she couldn't move her body, she tried searching for this annoyance by moving her eyes back and forth and darting them around the room. It seemed all so nonsensical as she tried desperately to figure out what was happening to her and how she got to this place, this dark room where he had left her all alone or so she thought.

She could feel her body rising up as if she was suspended from the ceiling, her feet not touching the ground. How was she doing this, how was she floating in mid-air? It was incomprehensible to say the least, but she wanted so desperately to understand.

She could feel her anxiety intensify and her heart begin to race. The noise above her seemed to have amplified even more so, mimicking her heartrate to an excruciating level, to the point of feeling as if her eardrums would burst and her heart would stop.

She heard something stir in the corner of the room and her eyes immediately shifted in that direction. From what she could make out, it was the silhouette of a man standing there and she could hear him whisper in the same cadence over and over, "What is truth and what is make-believe, what is truth and what is make believe?"

Who was this man, what was he talking about? She had to find a way to escape, she had to get the hell out of here.

The air in her lungs became restricted—she was struggling to breathe, gasping, desperate for air, and trying to yell out for help, wanting to plead for her life. She knew he would come back for her. She knew he would finish her off. There was no place she could hide anymore. He had finally found her.

She could feel his slimy hands on her body. She could smell his breath in her face. It was his responsibility to kill her and he had drilled it into her mind over and over again. She knew he would have to kill her in order to move on to his next victim. She was his Responsible Number Six and it was time for her to leave this earth.

The noise above her came to an abrupt stop and voices filled the room, now illuminated with bright light. She could feel hands on her chest pushing hard on it and the voices mumbling words she couldn't comprehend. It was chaotic for several minutes and then dead silence.

The police officer that was assigned to the patient in room 417 was still standing outside the door with arms folded over his overly starched uniform. He was alerted that a visitor by the name of Wendy Hill would be arriving within the hour and he watched her walk down the long hallway toward the guarded room. She introduced herself and handed him her credentials.

His expression was stern, as he glanced down at her license and then back up at the visitor and nodded, giving her clearance to enter the room. Her heart was pounding as to what she was about to encounter on the other side, bracing herself for the worst possible scenario.

She had been traveling all night taking the red eye from across the globe in hopes to arrive in Chatham in time before it was too late. She and her husband were celebrating their anniversary when she received the dreaded phone call that her sister was missing and possibly dead and now a heart attack, of all crazy things.

She stared at the face of this person she had known all her life and couldn't imagine what she had gone through and how she managed to survive from the hands of a maniac still at large in this small town. She was grateful she had made it to her sister's side before it was too late.

She sat there next to her hospital bed for several hours waiting, hoping she would come out of it and recover from this horrific incident. The doctors gave her a small percentage of surviving, however, she knew her sister and she would pull through. She was strong and had so much to look forward to.

"Kerry Ann, open your eyes. Please come back to us, we need you here."

Wendy rested her head on top of folded hands and allowed the tears to roll down her face. She attempted to call out her sister's name in hopes she would recognize her voice, reaching out to grab her hand.

Suddenly Wendy felt a squeeze and then her sister managed to speak. "Where am I? What happened?"

"You are in the hospital, Kerry Ann. You had a heart attack. It's me, Wendy, your sister. I am here with you."

"Wendy, it can't be you. He told me you were dead, he told me you went through the windshield of your car. You are not real are you? Are you truth or are you make-believe?"

"What are you talking about? Who told you I was dead? What does that mean—am I truth or make-believe? You are scaring me, Kerry Ann. You are making no sense."

She watched the monitors and Kerry's heart rate increased as she thrashed back in forth in her hospital bed. "I thought you were dead, Wendy, but he freaking lied to me. That sick bastard—he lied to me, he lied to me. He was here in the hospital. He tried to kill me last night. I saw him standing over me—I felt his hands around my throat."

"Kerry Ann, calm down. You have been through a lot. There was nobody here—you were protected. You are safe now. The police will catch this guy. I am here with you ... I am here. And I am truth."

CHAPTER THIRTY-ONE

Jake and Grace had already made a pact that they would stay at the crime scene on Briggs Way once the investigators had taken away all the evidence and dusted for fingerprints. Even though the crime tape is still up and this is technically still a crime scene, they had clearance—after all, it was their case.

They waited outside in the backyard on the lush grass and under the stately trees for what seemed like hours on end, not discussing their plan with any of the other blues. They were relieved when the last of the squad cars pulled away departing the scene, leaving them to their sudden urge to dig.

"You know, Grace, I am forced to say it again. I know you think that Mr. Foster is guilty of something, but I think you are wrong about him. He was just trying to find his wife's killer and you know from past experience that you would do anything for family—anything.

"And on a side note, I find you to be a bad influence sneaking around this house. This does not feel like normal protocol—it feels wrong somehow."

"It's not like we are treasure hunters, Jake. We are just being thorough and rifling through a closet or two inside. Searching this house isn't exactly breaking the rules of protocol. It makes perfect sense to me."

They stepped inside the house and immediately were hit with the first problem, which was the big hairy red dog staring them down. He was sitting in the kitchen panting, drooling his slobber all over the floor and waiting at his dog bowl for someone to toss in some kibble.

"He looks hungry," Grace said.

"Yes, agreed, he looks more than hungry. Do you think he plans on taking a bite out of my leg, because that would not be a good thing in my mind," Jake interjected.

"Don't be a wuss, Jake, I got this."

Grace walked over toward Bentley and put her hand in front of his nose letting him sniff her in hopes he would approve. His tail wagging, it seemed she passed the test, so she patted him on his head and told him he was good boy a couple of times in an unfamiliar cutesy voice Jake had never heard before. It didn't take her long to find his food in the pantry, gave him a healthy pour into his bowl, and now the first problem solved.

"Okay, vicious dog occupied, let's take a look around."

"Wow, impressive. Fighting crime on the streets alone and a dog whisperer. I couldn't be prouder. And—what exactly was that little girl voice I just witnessed?"

"Shut up and stop being such a smart-ass," Grace said, with a snarky tone.

She opened the first closed door past the kitchen and switched on the light. Jake followed behind her, scanning the room with his detective's eye on immediate alert. It was a small space, but appeared by the looks of the cluttered desk that it was one of the many rooms in this house that was utilized on a day-to-day basis.

The window was flanked with heavy lined draperies from ceiling to floor and matching fabric ties pulling them to the side, making it easy for the person sitting at the desk to admire the beauty of the backyard. In the middle of this incredible backyard stood that glorious tree that seemed to be the beacon from this room and most likely all the rooms and angles both inside and outside this house. Grace couldn't help but feel a little jealous as she had always wanted a place like this to retire in someday. Her personal oasis and, oh, yes, the bonus to be facing the Atlantic Ocean and beachfront and more of a bonus to actually get paid enough to own this so called oasis. *A girl can dream*, she thought.

Grace walked along the built-in bookcases, admiring the cherry wood and running her fingers along the smooth handcrafted workmanship. The library of books this couple had collected over the years was beyond impressive and she couldn't help but think they had to be worth a pretty penny. In between the books were an eclectic array of wooden figures perhaps brought back from their European travels. There were many travel photos from around the globe and, of course, the traditional family gatherings taken right here in this old house. She came across many photos of the once happy couple, which was the first time Grace had seen a photo of Kate—alive and vibrant—not through a clear plastic forensic evidence folder.

"What are the chances of finding anything remotely suspicious or curious at this point that the blues would not have already confiscated, Grace? You know for a fact that they have swept this place clean on more than one occasion now, and when Peter reported the bloody trail from his wife's murder a month or so back."

"You know it pisses me off that I wasn't there when they found her on the beach. It pisses me off even more so that I wasn't there to question her scumbag husband."

"You were not ready for that, Grace, as you were in the middle of one of your episodes and putting you in a small room with Peter Foster would not have been a healthy situation for you or Mr. Foster. I knew you would be fine, however, him not so much. Besides, you are up to speed now, so what difference does it make?"

"Yep. Lucky me. Up to speed and still no suspects. C'mon, Jake, let's move to the next room, since we didn't find anything questionable in here. Be careful though, as Fang is in the hallway waiting to attack those chubby ankles of yours." Grace laughed out loud and patted Bentley on the head on the way to the next room.

Jake's cell phone rang out for what seemed like a dozen times today from the same number since the sun came up this morning. He finally gave in and answered the call, interrupting their search of this massive amount of unnecessary square footage.

"Detective Elliott here. Who is this and what the hell do you want?"

Grace shot him a look of an immediate disapproval on his phone etiquette. Major fail in her opinion. She just shook her head and walked ahead into the next room, feeling somewhat sorry for whoever was on the line.

"Well, it's about freaking time, detective. I have been trying to reach you for days now. Left several messages with the weasel at the front desk at the precinct and I do believe by the tone of his voice, he was tired of taking my messages. I thought you were the lead detective on this serial killer case being broadcasted on the news every five minutes. What has happened to common courtesy of a returned phone call after twenty-four hours of the initial first message, detective?"

"I am going to repeat myself—who the hell is this?" Jake's face was now blood red and one of his hands clenched in a fist, ready to hit something.

"Let's just say I have something that will be of interest to you and that hot partner of yours."

"What's your name, smart-ass?"

"You can call me, Cabbie 47. And trust me, I am the real deal, the actual Cabbie 47. There seems to be an imposter cruising around this town, setting me up to face four concrete walls for life. I will get to that, but you might want to jot that down in that little notepad you keep in your top pocket. Am I right, Detective? It's there, isn't it?" He chuckled out loud at his own joke, knowing the truth of it at the detective's expense.

Jake ignored his comment while patting down his pockets, feeling around for his small notepad safe and secure, and then waited for more bullshit to spew out of this guy's mouth.

"Listen to me, detective and put me on speaker so your partner can hear, because I am sure she is within earshot. I have been set up and I am now fed up with the way I have been treated by the so-called police department. Since your boys have done a piss poor job of tracking down any leads, I took it upon myself to follow one of my own after my unfortunate detainment and being falsely accused of killing that girl found at the pier. I have strong evidence that will prove my innocence and you will have your killer behind bars and justice will be served. Meet me at the abandoned railroad tracks over on State Street in 30."

CHAPTER THIRTY-TWO

The detectives vacated the Foster's property within minutes of hanging up with the unforeseen caller. They made certain they secured the premises, leaving the owner's dog behind in full-on canine disapproval. His sad eyes penetrated right straight through to Grace's heart and Jake knew exactly what that meant in an instant.

"Oh here we go. I can predict what your next move will be, Grace. Your face says it all—you are so coming back to check on your new friend, Fang, aren't you?" Jake said, with a shit-eating grin on his face.

"Damnit! You can read me like a book, Jake. That really pisses me off. By the way, I am positive that the dog's name is Bentley, as I noticed it was engraved on his bone-shaped tag on his collar. You can gloat all you want as I really don't care. I am 100 percent sure on your assumption that I will be going back to check on Bentley. It appears his master is missing, so I have no other choice in this matter."

She stood at the passenger door, feeling annoyed as to why Jake had not unlocked the door, when she realized it wasn't actually locked. She rolled her eyes in her own embarrassment and pulled on the handle.

They took their seats, buckled up, and started the short ride to the old tracks where the caller directed them to meet up. They were both in agreement to not call this meet and greet into the station and took it upon themselves to answer the many questions of "why" later. It was now apparent they had a lead and had no intentions of letting him get away.

"How do you know that we are not being set up, Jake? Why wouldn't he give us his real name? Hell, we should have insisted that he divulge his identity. I mean this Cabbie 47 shit isn't going to cut it with me. Once we are face-to-face with this guy, I will be getting his name, address, Social Security number, blood type, and his entire family's DNA, including his dead relatives. They are all pissing me off."

"Seriously, Grace, you have been overly dramatic these days. I am anxious to see the evidence this guy has, as it might just lead us to the killer. So, chill, please."

"Yeah, you are right, Jake, about the evidence—not that I am being dramatic. This is my normal attitude. We shall see in a few minutes."

"Since we have a few minutes, I need to bring something up that I have not had a chance to discuss with you," Jake said with a nervous tone and rolled the window down a crack to get some ventilation in the small space.

"What is it, Jake—do share."

"When Peter Foster came down to the precinct, he and I had an in-depth conversation about his late wife's murder and were wrapping things up or so I thought, when he nonchalantly took a plastic bag out of his top pocket. He slid the questionable contents across my desk, as if he was offering me a stick of gum."

"Wait, wait, wait—you took in a piece of evidence from the one person I have been suspicious of this entire case? The sad pathetic widower was holding onto evidence to his wife's murder and you didn't tell right away? Jake, what the hell!"

"Grace, you have no grounds to give me shit about this or should I start calling you Nancy Drew? You were not available to me or anyone for several hours, remember? So, do you want to hear what I have to say or not?"

Grace let out a sigh and tapped her foot on the plastic floorboards of Jake's Cadillac, giving in to his need to share.

"Peter discovered this evidence when his dog, Bentley, returned home after being missing for over two weeks. He showed up out of the blue in the backyard, dehydrated and exhausted. The ribbon key as he called it for obvious reasons belonged to his late wife and was wrapped tightly around Bentley's collar. His wife had attached her house key to this ribbon and tossed it over her neck so she could lock the house behind her and do her morning run. What we just discovered from Parker, 'the asshole,' was there was a second key intertwined in the twisted ribbon that Peter did not recognize. This extra key sent him on a scavenger hunt through the entire house turning it upside down. He searched every square foot of that house—her closet, dresser drawers, but I would have to assume to no avail."

"Jake, *unnecessary* on the asshole comment. You need to give Parker a break."

"You need to give Peter Foster that same break," said Jake.

Giving it right back made him feel good, glancing over at Grace, and expecting a rebuttal. Nonetheless, she settled with a dirty look.

"Okay, Jake, let's stay on topic. You mentioned that Peter Foster turned that old house upside down searching for that secret. You do realize that everyone has secrets and whether or not they are in plain sight, inside a dark closet, or taped on the bottom of a dresser drawer, it doesn't matter, because eventually 'you' the hypothetical you, will find something to question. So, my 'you' question would be, where is this ribbon key now?

"I had it properly bagged, tagged, and logged-in to this case number and now its sitting in the evidence locker back at the precinct."

"I would like to take a look at this evidence immediately when we return to the precinct. I might be able to decipher what this key opens. I have a unique skill set, Jake, and you know it."

Jake pulled his old Cadillac onto the gravel road and drove cautiously toward the train tracks, doing his best to avoid the random potholes. The tires rolled over the uneven road expelling fragments of shell and rock, sending them bouncing up and off the rims and hubcaps as if someone was firing off a BB gun and using them as target practice.

The storm clouds were starting to form over the treetops, which was typical for this time of year. The rain would eventually turn to cold and the cold would lead to the dreaded snow.

Jake pulled the car up to the grade crossing signal, a signal that has not functioned in years. There was an abandoned train car on the tracks that had been used on many occasions as an artist canvas. Paint cans sat now empty and used for a colorful combination of art and obscenities.

Jake flipped on the windshield wipers to clear the mist of rain that was starting to come down from the storm that was brewing.

"I am starting to lose my patience with this guy. He'd better show," Grace said while drumming her unpolished fingertips on the dashboard.

A beam of headlights snapped on and lit up the front seat of Jake's car like a Christmas tree. Grace jumped out of her seat, grasping onto the door handle, ready for her escape.

They sat frozen in their seats waiting for this guy to make the first move. They could see him shuffling around in his truck, then his door flung open, and he slid out, making his grand entrance. He was average in height, had on a pair of dark jeans, a blue t-shirt, and a Cubs baseball hat.

Jake opened his car door and Grace followed suit, so now they were face-to-face with the caller.

"Let's skip the pleasantries and get right to it, shall we?"

"Wait a minute. What's your name, buddy? This Cabbie 47 shit isn't going to fly with me. We need to see some identification."

"Not necessary, detective, this town is small, and you will figure it out eventually. Keep in mind, I am the innocent one that has been set up and that doesn't fly with me."

He pulled out his cell phone from his back pocket and hit **play** on the video in question. The nameless informant turned the screen around to show the detectives and together they stood there and watched the horrific scene unfold. The rain was now pouring down hard, stinging their skin and soaking their clothes. Nonetheless, it didn't seem to faze them. They stared at the grainy video and for the next two agonizing minutes the realization had set in for the first time that they have seen the face of the serial killer—otherwise known as "the Responsible One," the one who has been killing these innocent people and baffling authorities for weeks.

"Oh my God, Jake, that's our killer—not suspect, but killer. This video proves that this sick psychotic bastard who has been walking around literally in our own backyard this entire time has been caught in the act. This case is finally solved. He will not be able to kill again," Grace said, her voice quivering and her body now visibly trembling.

"Yes, he has been identified, but then again, we still need to find him. There is a chance he could still get to his next victim before we can stop him. Case not closed—murderer not behind bars, not yet. It's now time to call this in."

CHAPTER THIRTY-THREE

The Responsible One stood inside the phone booth on the corner of an abandoned gas station located on the outskirts of the small town he had been terrorizing. He dropped in a quarter into the slot and punched in the number to his informant, the punk he bribed or more like suckered into being his accomplice. It didn't surprise him that this guy was not only a dirty cop, but a dirty cop that would agree to do anything to quench the addiction he craved daily, even if it meant covering up for a serial killer.

He found it easy to manipulate this guy, his informant, as he knew from his own experience that most people that have a drug addiction can maintain a job, pay bills, and glide through the day knowing that they can reach out at any time and grasp onto the grand prize without getting caught. It was obvious he was willing and eager to take candy from the "candy maker" in exchange for what he needed to get to his next victim. It was undeniably a win-win. He was using him as his eyes to go beyond the crime scene tape, where his fingerprints, his signature, and his clues had been left there in plain sight for all to see, yet still not revealed.

Waiting for the connection, he realized the door to this archaic piece of shit was hanging by a thread, as well as his psychological solidity. With an attempt to fix it, he ended up kicking it off the rusty hinges and putting it out of its misery, yet amplifying his anger to an entirely new level. The perspiration was dripping off his heavy-set stature, as he speculated in this moment how in the hell he was able to squeeze himself inside this antiquated tin box; on the other hand, how he was going to get out.

He had spent many grueling hours convincing himself that he had created a cohesiveness to his day-to-day activities to all that might take notice. He was more than confident that he blended into society, making it believable for most anyone including his employees to think he was sane and not guilty of anything but hard work. Hell, he even convinced his victims he was a normal person, not some psychopath on the ready to murder anyone who might be in his way. How else would he have befriended them and become a part of their lives until it was their day to die, the day he selected for their last breath of air. He found it challenging to see just how long he could string them along and coax them to where he wanted them to be in any given situation. He could recall that all of them didn't go as planned, nonetheless, he did his diligence to succeed with the inevitable.

The phone rang twice and even though the connection was faint, he could hear voices muffled in the background, but then not the voice he recognized. There was dead air, which meant his informant was surrounded by the enemy. He could envision them rushing around the precinct, rifling through the stacks of overstuffed files, desperately searching for that missing piece of the puzzle, yet nothing fit.

The Responsible One slammed his hand hard up against the glass interrupting the painful silence between them and screaming into the receiver the only request that was on his mind, "Did you get what I asked for?"

"I can't talk—but I need to meet you. I am desperate."

"You don't get to be desperate; I control you, remember? Did you get the shot? It better be in focus and not that blurry shit you sent me last time. Anyone could have taken that last photo and you call yourself a professional, how disappointing.

"Your assignments have not been difficult—even a four-year-old could have done a better job. You will get your payment for your nasty addiction when you get me the photo I asked for. Do not make me beg—it's that simple."

"Hold on. Give me a minute to find a private location so nobody is in earshot."

His accomplice walked out the back door of the precinct without any questions or looks from his colleagues. After all, they were buried in their own case files and completely self-absorbed.

He stepped into the alleyway and found a place to stand where he wouldn't be seen. Directly across from him was a row of overflowing trashcans. He found himself pulling his shirt up over his nose for a second as the stench caught him off guard.

There was a homeless guy rummaging through its contents while humming a show tune. It was obvious that he was three sheets to the wind as he watched him slug something out of a brown paper bag while adding the treasures he found into his grocery cart with the rest of his worldly possessions. This guy could care less about what Parker was doing there. Hell, he didn't even know himself where he was or what he was doing.

Parker was trying to figure out what to say to the psychopath on the phone, his mind spinning out of control and hoping to not get caught. It dawned on him, that he didn't care at this point if they found out he was involved. He just wanted his drugs and then he would just fade into the background and go on with his pathetic fake life. His golden boy reputation would be tainted, but he was willing to risk it all.

"What the hell, Parker, you need to get this done, I trusted you to make this happen and now too much time has passed between my victims and too many interruptions.

"It's not my fault you have been hauling around dead weight in the trunk of your car. And—I don't want to know what you did with that guy, so save it. They will figure it out when the birds start circling above you and then you are on your own. You need to understand that I am surrounded by cops 24/7 and the timing needs to be on point. Your next victim has been difficult to track down, so I have someone else in mind. I think you will be pleased who I chose for you, as it will bring back some vivid memories. Why bring you the photo when I can deliver her to you directly and in person. In exchange my payment is COD, if you will."

"What happened to the small meek weasel I hired for this job? I must admit you surprise me, Parker. And now I am intrigued with this unusual twist in who is playing the negotiator. You are one desperate piece of shit and you better not be blowing smoke. At this point, I am not quite sure if you are trying to be good cop/bad cop here, but I know for a fact you can't be both. You better deliver me someone or I can promise you that I will turn this entire murder investigation around, and you will be the one facing the four concrete walls of a prison cell.

You now have my full attention and I will look forward to digging up any memories from the graves of my past. Who could this person possibly be? Do tell."

"Detective Grace Harper—you knew her sister, right?"

CHAPTER THIRTY-FOUR

It was close to midnight by the time Jake dropped his partner off at her house. It was the second time he had set his eyes on Grace's place of residence as he had only seen it from the street. She never asked him to come inside and he never brought it up. Her personal life seemed more like a mystery to him and on more than one occasion he would try and get answers from her about her past besides her sister's traumatic death, however, she kept things locked up tight in that vault of hers.

Still numb from what they had just witnessed at the train tracks, Grace opened the heavy door to the Cadillac, but before she could make her way out, Jake grabbed her wrist, stopping her and not letting her go without offering some positive assurance.

She looked at him square in the face, her eyes cloudy and glazed over from tiredness and the shock of the evidence they had just witnessed together.

"Hey," Jake said softly. "We will find this cigar smoking son-of-a-bitch, Grace. It won't be long now—this case will be closed, and he will be behind bars for good."

He released her wrist and they said their goodbyes. Then she walked up to her porch and keyed the front door. She peered through the slats of the front window blinds and watched Jake pull away, closing off the outside world in one twist.

She lived alone by choice. No want or need for a roommate situation or any type of animals to come home to, not even a goldfish. Her mom always said she was an independent woman and she liked it that way.

Grace inherited this small piece of heaven from her late grandmother. She had the privilege of taking care of her Grandma Rose for so many years inside these faded light blue walls, Seaside blue, appropriately fitting as the name of the paint color her grandma had mentioned on more than one occasion.

Grandma Rose was an artist by trade, self-taught, and she used the sea and the life beneath it as her muse. She would sign her canvases with a small pink rose and comment out loud for anyone who might be listening that the rose was good enough as her signature and the folk that would purchase her art would have to figure out who was behind the easel with the paintbrush. She was both humble and talented.

Some of the local stores still displayed her work and on occasion would sell a piece or two and donate the small amount of cash to whatever cause they supported. This way her grandma was always giving her talent and love for arts and making a difference in someone's life.

She could still hear her laugh and see that amazing smile of hers as they were both infectious and now 100 percent convinced, she had inherited both. Funny how family traits are passed down from one generation to another. Grandma Rose was a kind, sweet and somewhat of an ornery woman who she will forever admire. For her grandma, the sea was her muse and for Grace, her grandma was.

Grace changed into her sweats and threw her hair up in a ponytail. Even though she was exhausted, she was too wired to sleep at this point. She opened the door to her office, giving it a push a couple of times as the old paint would sometimes stick to the door jam. Old house, old doors, old everything. She leaned in over her desk, searching blindly for the pull chain to the desk lamp that once belonged to her dad, the one thing she held onto after he abandoned his family so long ago. She yanked on the chain twice and the low wattage lightbulb illuminated the only subject matter that encompassed every inch of her desk. For the past 18 years, it has turned into an obsession in more ways than one.

There were stacks of files filled with police reports, albums stuffed with photos, and newspaper clippings of the news media circus daily attempt to write front-page news to grab their readers. It didn't take long for the articles about her sister's tragic murder to get pushed deeper and deeper between the pages until eventually there was nothing to write, nothing to report. They seemed to enjoy twisting their words to impress their readers with their journalistic speculation of who killed her sister and ruined their lives forever. The headlines hit the papers daily for weeks on end in a constant reminder written in well-ordered justified columns that it was a cold case, an endless reminder forever in print that she lost her sister to murder and her parents under the circumstances.

Grace moved the files around like she did every night, hovering over the contents like an overprotective mother. She picked up one of the files to stack it on top of the disorganized chaotic system she manifested, and in doing so, she accidentally dumped the contents to the floor. She bent down sort of groaning and grumbling of the aches and pains of the late hour and started gathering the contents, sweeping them toward her until something caught her eye. Leaving the pile on the floor, she stood up and held onto this one photo she recalled confiscating or more like stealing from the detective that was assigned to her sister's case so long ago. She held it under the light and saw something she hadn't noticed before—something that the detectives never brought up to her parents and she was too young and naïve to have questioned. Her sister's clothes were lined up on a stainless-steel table, like something you would see inside a morgue. Each of the items were strategically placed and numbered from shirt to shoes. Safety pinned to her pants was a handwritten note of a statement she had recognized somehow. The handwriting looked familiar, but she couldn't quite place it … until …

She gasped, bringing her hands to her face and covering her eyes in shock and disbelief. She found herself feeling faint and collapsed onto her desk and then down to the cold hardwood floor, bracing her fall with her hands. Tears filled her sad eyes and spilled onto her cheeks as she tried to comprehend what she was looking at. She tried to grasp what she was seeing, and if there was truth behind it.

"Oh, my god! Oh, my god!" she shouted over and over at the top of her lungs, wishing now that someone was here to help her, someone was here to hold her up and comfort her emotions. This couldn't be true, this is not happening. "Oh, my god," she cried out again, pulling her knees into her body to comfort herself the best she knew how. She stared at the photo and her instinct was to reach out to Jake, reach out to someone, anyone.

CHAPTER THIRTY-FIVE

The cell phone on Grace's nightstand lit up, buzzing, beeping, and gyrating in circles until she managed to reach over to silence it, fumbling in the dark to quiet this unexpected interruption and put her out of her tired misery. She held the phone in her hand and did her best to focus on the digital time stamp.

"Three a.m.!" she blurted out in disbelief.

She shot straight up and looked at her phone at the incoming missed calls and the phone went off again in her hand startling her with a jolt.

"Okay, this better be good. Who and the hell is this?" she demanded with a shaky raspy voice.

"Grace, it's Parker. I need your help."

"Parker, what the hell—it is the middle the night. Your call scared the crap out of me. This can't wait until normal hours whatever that might be?"

"I need you to come with me, right now. I will pick you up. Grace, it's important. You are going to want to see this."

"Why can't you ask one of the blues on nightshift for backup?"

"Grace, you are my backup."

"Fine, come get me. I will text you my address."

Grace groaned at the thought of having to get up and function at this ungodly time of the night. She slipped into the same damp clothes she had on earlier that she had draped over the chair next to her bed, then pulled the drawer open to her nightstand and took out her 9mm Smith and Wesson and checked the magazine and layed it on her bed. She threw on her jeans, jacket, boots, and headed for the front door.

She heard the rumbling engine of Parker's Jeep pull up to her house and a text announcing his arrival buzzed in her phone. She headed straight to the street, not giving him much time to think about coming up to the door. Not a chance that was happening.

Parker leaned over from the driver's side and pulled up the lock button. She took her seat next to the forensic photographer with the urgent middle of the night show and share.

Grace buckled in and looked over at Parker, expecting an instantaneous explanation behind this urgent phone call and drive to God only knows where. Instead, he said nothing and hauled ass down the street.

She had never seen this side of Parker before, this dark, expressionless, almost sinister air about him, which was out of character to say the least. He seemed more than off, however, she didn't really know him that well to judge his character traits.

"What's going on, Parker—you look different, pale, even sweaty. Have you been drinking?"

"No, I haven't been drinking. What kind of question is

that, Grace? Just sit tight and you will find out in a few minutes where we are going."

"No, you need to fill me in on what is going on right now. That is how it works in the department, Parker—you are aware of this protocol."

"Yes, perhaps you are used to that, Grace, however, that is not the case tonight."

"I don't quite understand, perhaps it's the late hour, however, I am not comprehending. You are supposed to be a professional forensic science investigator that should be investigating the murders, alongside all of us that make up the department here in Chatham. You are responsible for reporting the dead bodies you find, suspects in question, found evidence you know, the simple things that make up an investigation. One of the reasons you have woken me up at this late hour. So where are we going? I demand you to tell me, now, not later!"

He abruptly slammed on the brakes, causing them to skid off the road. Grace braced herself for the impact, as they came just inches from crashing into a fence that was running parallel to the road.

She sat there motionless and in shock. Not giving her much time to process, Parker grabbed hold of both her wrists and pulled them in close to him, squeezing as hard as he could.

"Grace, look at me. Tell me that I now have your undivided attention, because I would be very disappointed if I did not. Do I?"

Grace glared into Parker's eyes and nodded yes to his question. She was terrified and had never seen this side of him in all these months they had worked together. He was desperate and overly anxious, his personality had been altered from this calm and collective demeanor to an enraged maniac and to her, now a complete stranger.

"You, detective, need to wait for your precious answers. There are just times that you need to be patient and wait—you and your almighty uppity bullshit that you spew out daily, which makes me sick. Using your sister's death, so those around you feel sorry for you. That is always the way with you, demanding, snapping your fingers at people, and wanting instantaneous answers when sometimes, detective, you need to shut up, listen, and wait. Most people don't get what they want—that is the truth behind it, so, my advice would be to accept it."

He squeezed her wrists harder, his eyes fixed on hers. She managed to free herself from his grasp and then checked her waist, feeling around for her weapon.

"Leave it, Grace. Don't even go there with me. What—you are now afraid of me, because I am freaking out? C'mon, Grace, I have seen you freak out on the job many times, having those little episodes that I hear the guys talking about behind your back. I would suggest you trust me. You can trust me—believe me, you need to trust me."

"I will never trust you again, Parker, you can mark my words."

He took off down the road, once again turning toward the train tracks. He accelerated the gas and was doing close to 70 mph and showing no mercy in slowing down. There was nobody on the dark streets at this hour, and why would there be?

Grace was holding onto the handle of the Jeep, processing what was happening and taking into consideration her choices at hand to escape or ride this out. At this speed, there would be no doubt in her mind that she would be killed on impact.

Parker hit the locks on her door and increased his speed driving erratically, swerving on and off the road and eventually making a sharp turn toward the old storage facility now abandoned and condemned.

She glanced down on the floorboards of the Jeep and could see a plastic bag. She grimaced at the thought of it, as to how she would manage to pick it up without Parker seeing her. She could feel her body heat up and her hands start to visibly shake, deciding to go for it. She reached down and grabbed the small transparent bag by the corner pulling it up slowly and laid it in her lap. She strained her eyes to see what was written on the bag, recognizing the markings and coding that it was clearly police evidence.

She could see the contents, the ribbon with the key tied to the end, the piece of evidence that Peter Foster turned over to Jake just hours ago.

Infuriated beyond description, she held up the plastic bag in front of Parker's face, catching him off guard and blocking his vision and causing him to swerve off the road once again and this time crashing into some underbrush. Their bodies whipped forward as the seatbelts were digging into them and she felt her body slam hard up against the dashboard. Parker hit his head on the driver's side window, leaving him dazed and in shock.

"Are you out of your mind, Grace?" he managed to spew out. "What the hell are you trying to pull? Are you trying to get us killed?"

"That question comes straight back to you, Parker. Why

do you have freaking police evidence in your possession? I am demanding you tell me right now."

Stunned at her move, he did his best to get his bearings, feeling his head and checking for blood. He glanced over at the closed storage door, making certain it was the right one and it was still secure with the padlock. Parker grasped her face in his hands squeezing it hard and then twisted her body toward the warehouse door they were about to enter.

She resisted his strength, however, he gave her no choice. Her eyes bounced back and forth, focusing on the door in question and then noticed the vehicle sitting at the opposite end of the warehouse. It was obvious they were not alone, as she could see the silhouette of a man in the driver's seat and once he spotted them, he started driving toward them, inching up slowly and revving the engine with every inch. She had chills running up and down her spine and could feel her body start to tremble. That was him, it had to be.

"Grace, hand me the plastic bag and get out of the vehicle. Do it now and make no sudden moves. It's time to see what is behind door number three."

CHAPTER THIRTY-SIX

Parker grabbed onto Grace's arm and shoved her rigid body toward the abandoned storage warehouse. She unwillingly stumbled over the rough terrain, tripping over her own feet, while objecting distinctly to the man walking beside her, the man she thought she knew as her friend, her colleague. The desperate pleas of her own voice echoed in the quiet damp air, a terrifying sound that she hardly recognized as her own.

The questions of his motives firing off in her in mind as to why he would bring her to this godforsaken place, this dark, broken-down dilapidated dwelling that seemed sinister and evil from where they stood. It looked like a crime scene that should be investigated—not taken to against her own judgment and will.

Her eyes shifted from the ground up, attempting to focus on the intended destination, casting her eyes on the sinister dwelling with the uncertainty of what was about to happen behind closed doors.

There were rows of garage-style storage units lined up, maybe six, three on each side. A couple of the doors were smashed in and off the tracks leaving the contents exposed. The door to which he was taking her had a rusty plaque dangling from a chain and swinging from side-to-side in the night breeze. There were numbers engraved on the plague she recognized, B12118, but why? Her mind was spinning as she processed this entire scenario desperately trying to remember. Why did she recognize these numbers, the plaque, this god-awful place? Suddenly, it all came flooding back in an instant.

"Oh, my God," she shrieked out loud, realizing that this was the abandoned warehouse that Kerry Ann told her about. She said, he was behind the silver doors, this was the place the killer took her—behind the silver doors.

"Parker, we can't go in here. It's not safe. We need to call for backup and I desperately need to tell you something, something that I discovered last night."

She turned toward him and looked directly into his bloodshot eyes; his hands still gripped onto her arm, but he didn't let up, not for a second.

"I think I know who killed my sister, I think it's the same guy that is killing these women in Chatham and I would have to believe that he is sitting in the taxicab staring us down at this moment. He is watching us, Parker. Are you listening to me? He is the cigar smoking son-of-a-bitch, the Responsible One that murdered my sister eighteen years ago in the basement of my family home and all these women in this town. You have to believe me, Parker. I am pleading with you at this point. This is beyond my intuitions—this is fact."

She could hear his heavy erratic breathing and watched him flounder and shift his body from side-to-side, growing more agitated and impatient with the circumstances. With that response, she is now more than ever convinced she is his prisoner and offering her in exchange for something. She wanted him so desperately to do the right thing and call for backup—she wanted this to be over.

"It's time to go inside, Grace."

He pulled the ribbon out of the plastic bag and used the smaller of the two keys attached to it to open the padlock, carefully lifting it up and setting the lock down on the ground. He looked up for a split second at the taxicab and the man in the driver's seat flashed the headlights at him, just once as if he was signaling him for the go ahead. He then lifted the door to the storage unit and together, they stepped inside and Parker closed the door behind them.

The room was dim and there was a distinct smell of soot and dead rodents that permeated the air, so pungent it did not go unnoticed. It was obvious the strong odor was coming from the stacks of discarded crates and soggy boxes that lined the perimeter of the concrete walls from floor to ceiling. Some of the contents were spilling out of the cracks and crevices of the long-forgotten belongings of someone's past. Glimpses of fragmented china, old clothes, and stuffed animals that were once loved by the arms of a child.

A shaft of light was coming from a crank window in the upper left-hand corner that was casting a thin glow onto this godforsaken hell hole. A hell hole she would have never thought she would be subjected to, as this in her mind could only be a scene from a horror film, not her reality.

In the murky shadows of this insignificant square footage,

she could see a chair leaning up against the back corner and between a row of boxes. At first, she thought her eyes were playing tricks on her until she realized the chair was occupied. There was a man slumped over, a man she recognized to be Peter Foster. His shoes were off and sitting next to him lined up neatly, as if his captor placed them in a closet or on a shelf.

Grace managed to free herself from Parker's grip and rushed to his side, calling out his name and shaking him frantically, trying to wake him from his unconscious state. His hands were tied and his clothes were soaked with sweat. Grace untied him immediately, still trying to wake him, repeating his name over and over.

"He isn't dead, Grace, just drugged, I am assuming, or maybe he hit him over the head. I wouldn't worry too much about it. He obviously isn't stuffed in the trunk of a car anymore," he added with a shrug of his shoulders.

"Is this what you wanted to show me, Parker? Did you have something to do with this?"

Grace stood up turning her body toward Parker. She was now convinced he was involved in these murders and he had betrayed her, Jake, and the entire force.

"You have been a part of this the entire time, haven't you, Parker? You are a bad cop—how could you? Explain yourself! Is this some sort of collaboration between you and the killer? What's in this for you?"

Her eyes searched the claustrophobic space for a weapon of sorts, knowing in her gut she had the upper hand and could pull her gun out at any given time. She waited with bated breath for his ingenious answers to her list of questions.

Her teeth were clenched and her hand on her side arm at the ready, when she realized he was not offering up shit.

Parker stared at Grace directly into her eyes, as he could feel the tension and anticipation of her want for the answers to her well-thought-out questions, her interrogation of sorts, yet he had nothing to say, nothing to give. He just stood there and stared deep into her eyes straight to her soul.

Grace shook her head in disgust and thorough disappointment. "You know, Parker, I truly thought highly of you and had your back all these months. Even when my own partner questioned your integrity, I backed you a hundred percent. I even thought you were attracted to me. But Jake was right all along —you are an asshole."

"I wouldn't flatter yourself, Grace, uptight women are just not my type. And, oh, by the way, I would get ready if I were you, because he's here."

The silver door lifted, sending the wheels grinding along on the track, stopping hard first and then bouncing back and forth sending a God-awful screeching sound ricocheting off the walls. In the shadows stood the man from the taxicab, making his grand entrance known. The red flames from his cigar illuminated in the darkness, as he took a long drag of his fat stogie and let out a stream of white smoke, sending it circling above him like an ominous cloud. This man, this psychopath they had been investigating all these weeks, was now standing before her by stepping inside what he referred to as his domain, his hideout, the 12 x 12 to which he brought his victims, his known domain.

Confidence was oozing out of every pore on his body—he

was seemingly in control of the situation at hand. He was responsible for what was about to happen behind the silver doors marked B12118.

CHAPTER THIRTY-SEVEN

"I want to be the first to welcome you to my home away from home. Do you like what I did with the place?" He let out a chuckle and then took a corner of his white t-shirt and wiped off the nervous sweat forming on his forehead.

He took a couple of steps toward the detectives, giving a quick glance to his prisoner slumped over in the chair and then crossed his arms over his chest.

"You know, I find it interesting that you both act like big shot detectives, yet I have left many clues, wait, hundreds of clues at each crime scene and so far, you still have both been so stupid not to have figured it out. I left them in plain sight—the cigar wrapper in Kerry's car, the ribbon with the keys tied to the end wrapped around poor Bentley's collar. I find it so incredibly frustrating that you didn't find any of them. I gave them to you on a silver platter, practically handed them to you without any strings attached. It would have been quite the bonus at the department if you would have cracked this case. But here you are now. Bravo to you, you caught me. I applaud you, I do."

He leans close to Grace, his stale cigar breath and mouth pressed up against her ear. She shudders in disgust and chills and terror run through her body.

"I want you to know, Grace, that I enjoyed your sister's delicious lips on mine before she died and, oh, how much I enjoyed watching her in the distance at her little track meets after school and running on those cold snowy streets of Chicago. I take it you found the photo on your desk? I actually placed that on your desk weeks ago. Of course, you most likely second-guessed yourself as to where it came from. After all, it has been eighteen long years—one cannot recall everything from their past."

"Oh, and Peter sitting over there, slumped over like the piece of shit that he is—his wife was the first to die in this godforsaken, insignificant town. I convinced him that his lovely Kate and I were having an affair and that I had sent her love letters and hid them in his house. You know, he spent weeks searching for those friggin' letters and didn't bother to search the yard. They were there the entire time. I stuffed them inside one of those boxes Kate had stacked on end inside her closet, stuffed them inside the box, sealed it, and buried it in the yard next to the tree swing. I do believe Mr. Foster figured they just didn't exist, but he was quite wrong. Kate was so vulnerable and naïve to think I could love her, however, I am very convincing and good at what I do. I have to admit, that was entertaining."

"This is a game to you isn't it. You wanted to get caught."

"Of course, I wanted to get caught! Why would I have left the evidence? Why would I have convinced this asshole to bring you here? However, today is not the day. You might think you have caught me, Grace, but in actuality you are fair trade. You see, Parker's unfortunate addiction has overtaken his morals and values and turned him into a bad cop. You are my next victim, Grace, my Responsible Number Seven.

"For you, Parker, the only way you found out about the key is because I told you. What an idiot. How could you have not figured that out?"

Parker smirks at the Responsible One and moves in a few steps closer, grabs his arm, and twists it behind his back, holding it tight and then slaps the cuffs on him.

"You know, I might be an asshole and an idiot as you say, but I will always be a good cop, with no addiction other than putting serial killers behind bars. Makes me so very happy. And I can promise you that I am the only negotiator in this scenario. You will have no more victims. You are under arrest for multiple murders, you will be prosecuted and spend the rest of your life in prison where you will rot to death."

Grace stood in shock at what just happened and within minutes the cop cars flew onto the scene, lights flashing and sirens on surrounding the 12 x 12 they stood in. Jake gets out of the car and grabs hold of the Responsible One, opening the car door and shoving him inside.

"It's over for you. It will always be over for you."

It had been several weeks since they placed him inside that prison cell. In the beginning, he was assigned to solitary confinement until they moved him to a regular cell. They allowed him to have a few pieces of paper, whereas on most days he would write on the walls or anything he could find. It was always the same sentences written over and over in his nonsensical psychopathic mind of writing and at the end of each sentence, he added a number, always the same number. The number seven sometimes was written in numeric and sometimes written out as a word. He never spoke to anyone and would be escorted in chains from his cell block to the commissary and back.

The guards would take that dreaded walk down to his cell for the daily and nightly check and as always he would be scribbling something on the wall or the paper he was given. He would keep to himself, never communicating with the guards or other cellmates. He made certain he would never give anyone eye contact. In his mind, they didn't deserve his eye contact.

It was close to eleven o'clock and bed checks were running behind the normal schedule on this particular day. The prison guard on duty strolled down the long corridor, but his heavy footsteps didn't go unnoticed as he prepared to do his due diligence by shining his flashlight onto the cots and the faces of each prisoner that occupied them. However, when he arrived at the Responsible One's cell, the door was wide open.

He stepped inside the cell and saw the prisoner's chair was turned toward the door. His prison uniform was folded up and neatly placed on the seat.

Pinned to his shirt was a note ...

*Thank you for the accommodations, however,
I cannot stay, as I have responsibilities to take
care of ... I need to kill her, my Responsible
Number Seven, just like I killed her sister in
the cold damp basement.*

Other Titles by Julie Ann James—

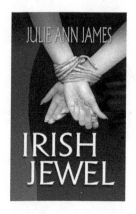

James takes her engaging characters to the gritty streets of Dublin, Ireland, where they become unsuspecting pawns in a twisted, tainted psychotic game of pure adulterated revenge from an unexpected and wicked mastermind. It is said to be true, that all families, have long-hidden secrets buried deep within their souls and locked away from all who might just go digging. Irish Jewel uncovers such a dark secret, so horrific that it could forever change lives when divulged. As the shocking truth surfaces, revealed for all to see, move across this chilling game board to determine where the grimy bread crumbs will end up. The suspense could kill you …

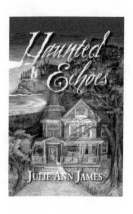

Sarah Reddington traveled to far-away Maine to escape the chaos of the windy city.   She wanted to concentrate on completing her novel and enjoy the peaceful quiet of the Atlantic's craggy shore.   Although she was the only registered guest staying in an elegant, but quaint Victorian Inn, subsequent events quickly placed her writing on hold.   The haunting cries that echoed around her made her question not only her own mortality, but made it difficult for her to decipher between fiction and insanity. This is an old-fashioned ghost story through-and-through that will keep you guessing until the last written word.

Julie Ann James lives in Sarasota, Florida. Her passion for words came at an early age and has inspired her to plant literary seeds enthusiastically all over the globe. She is the founder and publisher of The Peppertree Press book publishing company and *The Pepper Tree Literary Magazine*, an avid public speaker, a published children's author and mystery writer.

CPSIA information can be obtained
at www.ICGtesting.com
Printed in the USA
JSHW021348200920
7974JS00005B/25